THE Secret oF Ferrell Savage

THE Secret of Ferrell Savage

by J. Duddy Gill

ISBN 978-0-545-90857-3

Text copyright © 2014 by Jennifer Duddy Gill.
Illustrations copyright © 2014 by Sonia Chaghatzbanian. All rights reserved.
Published by Scholastic Inc., 557 Broadway, New York, NY 10012,
by arrangement with Atheneum Books for Young Readers,
an imprint of Simon & Schuster Children's Publishing Division.
SCHOLASTIC and associated logos are trademarks and/or registered
trademarks of Scholastic Inc.

12 11 10 9 8 7 6 5 4 3 2 1   15 16 17 18 19 20/0

Printed in the U.S.A.   40

First Scholastic printing, November 2015

Book design by Sonia Chaghatzbanian
The text for this book is set in ITC Souvenir Std.
The illustrations for this book are rendered digitally.

To Mary Ann Duddy,
who supports my dream
and laughs on cue

Acknowledgments

Thank you, first, to my sister, Mary, whose seventh-grade diary was the best book I ever read as a kid, and her honest words were what inspired me to write my own.

Thanks to Meghan Gates, who introduced me to Alferd Packer and then read the manuscript before anyone else. Thanks to my Weird Martian Gnomes, Christy Lenzi and Elizabeth Reimer, who share this journey with me. Robin Prehn, a special thanks to you for being the best writer friend another writer could have. The story couldn't have come this far without the critiques from brilliant writers Angela Ackerman, Jaye Robin Brown, and Deborah Halverson. And Jody Erikson, too, who isn't a writer but offered great suggestions and is all-around lovely. Thank you, Susan Wroble, who once read my first writing attempts and said, "Keep going!" and because of that, I did.

At Atheneum, I am grateful for the sharp eyes and creativity of Jeannie Ng, Kaitlin Severini, and Sonia Chaghatzbanian, who is also responsible for the adorable illustrations. And, especially, I'd like to thank my easygoing editor, Ariel Colletti, who loves Ferrell as much as I do, and Ruta Rimas, who also helped me raise him to be the fine young man he is today. Which leads me to an even bigger thank-you to the best agent in the world, Wendy Schmalz, who hung in there and found Ariel and Ruta for us.

There are no words, even in a thesaurus, that can express my love and gratitude for Mike, Jane, and Annie. Let's celebrate with pizza and kale!

Chapter One

EVERY WINTER, ON THE DAY AFTER CHRISTMAS, our town holds the Big Sled Race on Golden Hill. You'd think that after fifty years they would've come up with a better title for the event, especially since no one's used an actual store-bought sled in the race since before I was even born. It really should be called Get-to-the-Bottom-of-the-Hill-as-Fast-as-You-Can-on-Whatever-You-Want Race.

I've seen kids slide down on beanbag chairs, cafeteria trays, old refrigerator boxes, and even a torn-off car door. Last year Jerry Dunderhead built what he called a ski-ike by attaching a ski to his mountain bike. He tipped over at the starting gate, broke his collarbone, and that was that. Still, it could've been so awesome. Then there were the four high school seniors who built this thing that looked like a boat. It didn't go fast, so they had to jump out and push it most of the way, but it was cool. They had speakers hooked up to it, playing this song that I recognized but didn't know at the time, *The Ride of the Valkyries*.

Mr. Spinelli from Spinelli's Market has been the judge and timekeeper since my dad was a kid. He stands at the finish line with his gold pocket watch tied to his belt by a thick piece of string. One year he dropped that same watch into the deep snow and couldn't find it. So for the rest of the contestants' runs, he had to count "one Mississippi, two Mississippi." Some people complained he cheated when he declared his grandson, Franco Spinelli, the winner. And I saw that when Franco sped by with I ♥ MY GRANDPA painted on the side of his cardboard box, Mr. Spinelli got a little teary eyed, which would understandably slow down his Mississippis. Luckily, when the snow melted that spring, some kid found the watch and gave it back to Mr. Spinelli, and no one's accused him of cheating since.

Because you have to be at least twelve years old to compete, for the past eleven years my friends have been feeling an itch—worse than a scratchy sweater with no undershirt—to get their turn. It was like that every year. Twelve-year-olds are willing to bleed and break bones to win.

But not me. I didn't care about being the kid holding the big trophy at the end and watching all the other kids sniff up their tears and fake-clap. Being responsible for making my friends trudge all the way home, moping through the snow and dragging their home-built contraptions like they were roadkill, was not for me.

On Christmas day Mary Vittles stopped by to check out my under-the-tree stash and to see my "racing apparatus," as she called it.

Mary and I have known each other since we were in diapers. She and her mom live down the street from us, and when Ms. Vittles went back to work at the Colorado Inn, my mom offered to take care of Mary. Ms. Vittles said she'd pay Mom, but Mom insisted Mary was good for me, that she toughened me up. Besides, Mom liked having Mary around.

"Ms. Vittles has rent to pay and a little girl to provide for. It's a luxury for me to be able to stay home and take care of Ferrell," Mom always said. We weren't rich or anything, but Dad's job as senior librarian at the Golden Hill Library kept us well fed. Ms. Vittles never married Mary's dad, who ran out on them before Mary was even born.

"It's been tough on poor, sweet little Mary," Mom always said.

Don't be fooled by the words "sweet little Mary." She's kind of like honey mustard. The taste isn't bad, but you still feel like you got tricked into trying it. So, whether or not Mary and I were really friends was never a question for our moms. We're stuck with each other. I'm pretty sure I mean that in a good way. She's bossy and a know-it-all, but there are things I like about her.

I'll need some time to think about what they are, though.

When Mary arrived, Mom and I were clearing the dishes off the table.

"Mary, sweetheart, how about a little Christmas supper?" Mom offered even before Mary had taken off her coat. Mom pointed to the platter of leftover Tofurkey. "I'll fix it up with some cranberries and potatoes."

"No, thanks," Mary answered. She pulled off her hat and smoothed the static out of her brown, wavy hair. "My hypothalamus is sending signals that I've reached maximum consumption."

"Excuse me?" I asked.

"I'm full," she said. "Mom brought home some real turkey and a slice of ham from the restaurant. I made canned corn and sweet potatoes with butter."

I'd never eaten meat, but just hearing her say the words "turkey" and "ham" made saliva drip from my fangs. Even the butter, something else I'd never had, sounded so good and smooth. Just saying the word tasted sweet and creamy. Butter.

Mary tossed a chunk of Tofurkey to Buddy, my beagle. "All right, let's see what you built," she said. She headed toward the kitchen door that leads to the garage, but I didn't budge. She looked over her shoulder. "You're not coming."

I shrugged.

Mary turned around and put her hands on her hips. "No way," she said. "The race is tomorrow and you haven't built your apparatus yet! You have"— she looked at her watch—"less than ten hours to put something together."

She told me this as if I didn't already know.

"It's all up here," I said, pointing to my head. "I have a plan, it's brilliant, and you'll be surprised." I couldn't tell her my brilliant plan was to be a spectator.

She shook her head in disbelief. "You've got nothing."

She was right. The sled-making department in my head was empty.

"Let's go give yours another ride," I offered. "Just to see how the drain's staying plugged."

Mary was big on Dumpster diving. Back in the fall she had found an old metal kitchen sink—the kind with rounded edges—and she was determined to make it into a Big Sled Race winner. She'd cemented a plug into the drain hole, sanded it down, and waxed it up. Then she'd sat inside the sink and fallen over backward in the snow. I would have said, *Oh, well, it doesn't work,* and gone to find something else. But not Mary. She immediately began abdominal muscle exercises to help her hold her balance while curled up in a ball. After three weeks of training she tried it again. She sat in her silver sink, lifted her legs off the ground, leaned back just so, and zoom. The ride was supersmooth and steady. I hadn't seen the other contenders, but I still predicted she would win.

"I'm not worried," Mary said now as she leaned against the counter and folded her arms. She tried to make her brown eyes look sleepy and calm, but I didn't buy it. I know Mary. She hates losing, so she works super extra hard at everything she does. She was our school council's vice president, beating out the eighth graders, and last year her science project on heliotropes won second at state.

I rubbed my hand over my belly and was just considering a third piece of pumpkin pie for myself when Mary said, "So, did you get too busy and run out of time, or are you just being indolent?"

"Maybe," I said. I didn't know what "indolent" meant.

"Maybe what?"

"That second one," I said.

"Lazy," she said, throwing her hands hopelessly into the air. "It's like your mind just stops working sometimes."

I was used to Mary saying stuff like that. She always accused me of not paying attention or of being stuck in a daydream. When we do our homework, she calls me "airhead" or says, "Your brain's a muscle—use it or lose it." But it's not that I'm not trying; it's just that words, sometimes even full sentences, jump around the page when I read. And when I listen in class, it's the same kind of thing. Words float around close to my head but don't always make it in through my ears. I'd stopped trying to explain it to Mary years ago.

That night, after she called me lazy, something weird happened. I walked Mary home, because Mom makes me do that if it's after dark, even though it's only half a block away. When we got to her house, I said "Bye" and turned around to leave.

But she said, "Wait, I have something for you. Hold out your hand," and I did. She put a round yellow gumball into the palm of my hand. It was warm and sweaty from her own hand, which probably should have been kind of gross, but I thought it was cool. I held up the gumball to the light and saw that it had a face. Two eyes and heart-shaped lips, like a little kiss. I said "Thanks" and watched her walk up the steps to her front door.

I thought, *Wow, a gumball with a kissy face from Mary Vittles*, and then I popped it into my mouth. Only it wasn't a gumball; it was a marble. I'm lucky I didn't break a tooth, but I accidentally swallowed it. It hurt going down, and I felt it lodge itself in that space right between my heart and my stomach. As far as I know, it never came out, so it's probably caught there forever.

That night I watched *It's a Wonderful Life* with my parents, but I didn't hear a word Jimmy Stewart said. I thought about the marble, and for the first time ever, I was bothered that Mary had called me lazy.

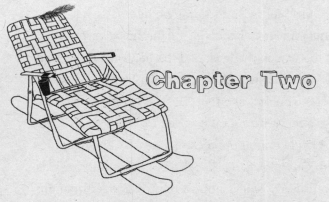

Chapter Two

MOM AND DAD DROPPED ME OFF ON THE ROAD at the top of the hill where all the other kids were making last-minute repairs on their sleds—or whatever you wanted to call them. Dad helped me pull mine out of the back of the station wagon.

"It's different," he said, looking it over. "I've never seen anything like it. Looks solid, like it'll give a smooth ride."

"Yeah." I nodded, hoping he was right. I'd never actually tried it out.

The night before, after rattling my brain to find an explanation as to why I was suddenly bothered by

Mary, I decided explanations were stupid and I didn't need one. I simply knew I had to do what I had to do.

So I went to the garage to scope out materials that would get me to the bottom of Golden Hill.

Quick and easy to slap together was what I was aiming for. First, I thought of the wheelbarrow. If I took the wheel, the legs, and the handles off, it could work. But that would be too much like Mary's sink, and she wouldn't like that. Besides, I didn't have the abs to keep it from tipping over.

I could empty out a cardboard box and decorate it with Sharpie markers, but that's what a lot of kids do, and Mary would not be impressed. As I continued to dig around, I found an inner tube, a couple of mismatched skis with the bindings broken off, a shovel, a plastic garbage can, a pair of sawhorses, and a purple recycle bin. All had possibilities, except for maybe the sawhorses. And then I spotted it—the perfect sled. An old lawn chair, the kind you lie down on—a lounge. I was going to lounge down the hill!

I pulled it off the nail it was hanging on and unfolded it. The frame was lightweight, and the part you lie on was made of these wide straps that were woven together. Whenever someone sat on it for too long on a hot summer day, the big gaps in the weave left checkerboard indents on their back. Once, when we had left it out, a big gust of wind carried it over the fence and into the neighbors' yard and into their dogwood tree, where it hung for weeks before another gust of wind finally blew it down and onto their lawn. The lounge had been through a lot.

I looked at its legs. There was no way they would slide across the snow without a little engineering. The mismatched skis! I could attach them to the legs with . . . not nails; they'd stick out and grab the snow and slow me down. And not rope, for the same reason. Superglue. We had a pack of three tubes on the workbench. I couldn't believe my luck. Everything was falling perfectly into place.

And so, there it was, sitting in the snow and winning the admiration of my dad. My lounge-sled, ready for its first run.

"Have fun, Ferrell. Don't worry about winning. Just go enjoy yourself," Dad said. He patted me on the back. "See you at the bottom of the hill."

"Good luck, honey. Don't forget to pull your hat down over your ears to keep them warm," Mom called to me from the front seat of the car.

I waved to my parents as they drove off, and then I dragged my sled toward the registration line. Something sharp poked me in my leg, and then I remembered the most important part of my racing apparatus. The decoration. I pulled a long, white feather from my pants pocket, smoothed it out, and stuck it in one of the small grommets on the lounge's frame. I had found the feather in a box in the garage, wrapped up in paper.

I remembered finding this same feather in a desk drawer in the living room when I was in first grade, and I had asked my dad if I could have it. I vaguely remembered him explaining that the feather had come from something called a pollypry, which had saved my mother's great-great-uncle from being killed. I hadn't cared much about the story behind it; I'd just wanted to jump off the couch and try one-wing flying. But Dad had pulled it out of my hand and said, "I better take that out to the garage before your mother sees it." The feather had thick, black crud at the bottom, where it had been attached to the bird; Mom had probably been worried about germs and diseases.

I stroked my hand across the top of the feather and thought about how cool it would look fluttering behind me on the hill. If it ever had carried diseases, surely those germs were dried up by now.

Next to the registration line, a crowd of kids had

gathered around some short guy. At first I thought they were making fun of him for wearing a blue-and-green plaid snowsuit, but as I got closer and heard the oohs and aaahs, I saw they were admiring his sled. I squeezed into the crowd to get a better look.

The sled had shiny, sleek, metal rudders; a polished wooden seat; and shock absorbers underneath.

"Suh-weet," I said.

"I know," the kid said. "I built it myself." His big-headedness was a little surprising, but, hey, there was no denying that this sled could be used in the army if we ever go to war in the North Pole.

"I call it the Titanium Blade Runner," he said.

More oohs and aaahs came from the crowd, including me.

"What about you?" he asked, looking at me. "What have you got?"

I had forgotten I needed to give my sled a name. I thought for a minute, and then it was obvious.

"Mine's called the Pollypry," I said.

The plaid-clad boy's jaw dropped, and his eyes got big. "Polly? Pry?" he sputtered, leaning toward me. "Why are you calling it that?"

I backed up, wondering what in the world had

made this kid so excited that he was about to jump out of his snowsuit.

I pointed to the feather, thinking that would make it obvious. "A pollypry saved my mom's great-great-uncle's life."

"No way! Are you a Packer?"

My head was starting to spin. First, we're talking about sleds, then we're talking about birds, and now he's asking me if I'm a Green Bay Packers fan?

"Gosh, no! I'm a Broncos fan all the way!" I said.

"Go, Broncos!" a couple of people shouted.

"Hey, I need to talk to you," the plaid kid said. But the crowd was getting thicker around his Titanium Blade Runner, and I got shoved out of the way.

I pulled off my hat and scratched my head. Wow, and people say I have an attention deficit disorder. That poor kid couldn't stay on one topic for more than half a sentence.

I put my hat back on, pulling it down over my ears like my mom had asked me to, and dragged the Pollypry toward the registration line.

"Hey, Savage!" My two best buddies, Coby and Eilio, called to me from the line.

"Whoa, that's cool," Coby said, checking out my lounge. "You'll be like a tropical Santa Claus sitting on that thing. Look, you've even got a drink holder!" He threw down his garbage can lid to get a better look.

Eilio ran his hand across the feather. "Is this supposed to catch the wind and make you go faster?"

Coby laughed. "How're you gonna control the thing?" he asked.

I hadn't thought of that. I lay down on it, and the feather towered over my head. I put my hands behind my head. "I'll lean side to side, like this," I said, and showed them.

"Unless you fall asleep," Eilio said.

I shut my eyes and pretended to snore, and they howled with laughter.

"Not too bad." That was Mary's voice. I opened my eyes, and there she was, hovering over me with her metal sink. "It suits you somehow."

I hoped that was a good thing. "Thanks," I said, just in case.

"The feather is a nice touch," she added.

Oh yeah, I definitely scored there!

"Dang, Mary. Yours is so shiny, it's blinding me," Eilio said. "How'd you get it like that?"

"Months of rubbing and polishing. Mine lacks aerodynamics, but it makes up for it in resistance. Feel." She held out her sink, and we all took off our mittens to stroke the bottom of it. "No friction between me and the snow."

"Where's yours, Eilio?" she asked. I was wondering the same thing.

"Aw, I'm just here for the swag," he said.

"Well, I'm here to win," Mary declared.

"You will," I said.

We all wished one another luck, and after I watched her walk away, I lay back down and let the warm sun heat up my down jacket. That's one of the things I love about Colorado—even when the ground's covered with snow, the air can feel like springtime.

I guess I lay there for too long, because by the time I got up and registered, I was number fifty-nine out of sixty contestants. Mary was fourth, and I watched her go. She curled her legs up tight and sailed down, smooth and sleek.

"Go, Mary," I whispered, making fists inside my mittens. But just before she got to the bottom, there was a loud pop, and her rubber plug went flying in the air. She came to a dead stop.

"Awwww!" the audience shouted, feeling her pain.

"Call a plumber!" a big kid yelled. Some folks laughed, but Mary shot the big kid a look that I'm sure made him feel like he'd just been flicked in the forehead. I've gotten many of those looks from Mary, and believe me, they sting.

She walked off the hill with her head hanging low, dragging her sink on its rope behind her.

Coby was number forty, and he zinged by on his lid. But he went off course and into the crowd, taking a couple of grown men down, like bowling pins. Jerry Dunderhead tried out his new and improved ski-ike, and this time he made it almost halfway down the hill before he hit a snow mound and was tossed into the air. He landed hard on his bike seat and then fell over, grabbing himself on the you-know-what. Every guy watching crossed their legs tight and said, "Aw, oh, oww!" Jerry was carried off with the help of his mom and his little sister.

Lots of kids had made their marks on this hill—some of those marks not so pleasant—and now it was my turn. I looked at the finish line, way down below. My hands were sweating inside my mittens. It was rare that I ever had butterflies, but there they were, flying around in that space between my stomach and my heart, where the kissy-face marble was lodged. But I also had this other weird feeling. Something I'd never felt before.

I wanted to win.

I wanted to shred that hill and get the big trophy. And when I got the big trophy, I knew exactly what I'd do with it. I would give it to Mary.

I sat up on the lawn chair at the gate, which wasn't really a gate at all (it was just two stakes stuck into the ground). I leaned forward, waiting for Mr. Spinelli to pop the cap gun. I spotted Mary below in her teal-blue hat.

Then *bam*! Mr. Spinelli's gun went off.

I pushed against the stakes with my hands and then reclined all the way back, stretching my neck just enough to catch a glimpse of the pollypry feather bending backward, like a palm tree in a hurricane. I kept my legs straight, my arms at my sides, and my toes as pointed as possible inside my boots. Then I tucked my chin down and closed my eyes tight. The sun was shining in my face so bright that I couldn't have opened my eyes if I'd wanted to. Then I heard a rip. Then a bigger *riiiip*, and the next thing I knew, the Pollypry had sucked me in and swallowed me whole. I was caught in the bowels of the lounge, digested by the straps and metal frame.

What happened next is all a blur to me, and everyone in town seems to have a different version of the

same story. But when I put them all together and aver-
age them out, the gist seems to come down to this: At
about fifty feet from the top, I was still building up speed
when suddenly I vanished—just disappeared—and no
one knew where I'd gone. The sled was airborne, flying off without me. But when the crowd finally spotted
me on the hill, I was rolling, spinning, cartwheeling,
and even did a backflip. All I know for sure is that I
was twisted and mangled, and at one point I felt my
knees hit the back of my neck. I rolled, and rolled some
more, the world spinning—turning snow white, then
sky blue, then back again—until I reached the bottom
of the hill. Some people say the whole episode seemed
to take hours; others say it happened in less than two
Mississippis. Poor Mr. Spinelli forgot to look at his
watch, so we'll never know.

When my body reached the bottom of the hill,
I heard all the screaming moms—mine above all the
others—and people yelling things like "Whoa!" and
"He's a goner!" and "Hey, Dad, I want to try that!"

Then the crowd was completely quiet, and I figured the last guy must've been coming down. I lay
on the ground, spitting out snow and doing a quick
inventory of my limbs, nose, and butt, making sure
all those parts that should have been broken weren't.

Then I shook myself, turned my head around so that the world was upright again, and scrambled to my feet.

Still nobody moved. Puffs of white clouds had stopped coming from their mouths. It crossed my mind that maybe during the fall, I'd developed the power to stop time. I was thinking I should take Coby's dad's beloved snowmobile for a quick spin, since he was frozen and all. But instead the crowd burst into an explosion of wild cheers and a thumping of applause that was muffled because they still had their mittens on. So time hadn't stopped at all. Disappointed, I looked around to see what all the commotion was about. Maybe the next sledder was doing triple axels or something.

But nobody was coming down. The cheers were for me, and within seconds I was bombarded with hugs and handshakes. Some people were crying, and others were thanking God that I was alive.

Mr. Spinelli pushed back the crowd and had me stand on a podium, which was really just the bottom of an old, half-melted snowman. He announced through his loudspeaker, "Ladies and Gentlemen, I believe we've witnessed a miracle." He looked up at me on my snowman-torso podium and whispered,

"You're lucky you're not going to your own funeral tomorrow, son."

I wasn't sure how to respond, so I said what my mom taught me to say when I was stumped for words. "All righty," I said to Mr. Spinelli.

"I present to you," he yelled to the people, "our own Ferrell Savage, Golden Hill's great survivor! Wave to the people, son."

At first waving made me feel like a show-off. But since I hadn't actually won the race, there was no reason for anyone to have hard feelings on account of me. There should've been no moping kids, nobody sniffing up the tears of a loser.

I searched the crowd for Mary, and there she was, heading home. She yanked on the rope until the sink slid in front of her. Without looking back, she stomped in her boots, making a deep gash in the snow and kicking everything in her way, including her kitchen sink.

Chapter Three

FOR THE REST OF THE WINTER BREAK I COULDN'T go anywhere without someone saying to me, "Hey, aren't you that dude who almost got killed on the hill? You're a true survivor, man."

All the attention blew me away, in a good way, but I still wished I'd gotten the trophy for Mary. Or, better yet, I wished Mary had gotten it. She's used to winning; after all, she wins everything.

As angry as she seemed to be about losing, I wondered if she thought my fall was awesome, like everyone else did. Just in case she tried some big vocabulary on me, I used a thesaurus to look up and memorize big words for "amazed." I imagined she'd say something to me like, "I'm astonished! Your exploits have left me flabbergasted and astounded." Sometimes she says stuff and I'm not sure if I've been complimented or insulted, so I try to be prepared.

On the first Thursday back to school, I got on the bus, which made stops at the elementary and middle schools. As always, Mary sat on the left side of the seat, smack-dab in the middle of the row. Sarah Yellen sat next her. I grabbed the seat behind them, next to a little blond-haired girl with an Astro Boy lunchbox. I cleared my throat real loud, so Mary would know I was there. She closed the book she was reading and looked out the window.

Sarah twisted around in her seat. "Hey, Ferrell! I saw you in the newspaper," she yelled over her iPod's music. "I wish I'd been here to see you instead of at Disney World."

"Gosh, thanks," I said. I knew she didn't hear me, though. She turned back around, bobbing her head to her music.

Mary kept looking out the window, pretending she didn't notice me. Ever since we'd started middle school, she had this new thing she'd do. She'd get mad at me, even when I hadn't done anything. It was very confusing, and, to tell the truth, it was annoying. She wouldn't ever tell me why she was mad; she'd simply ignore me. Sometimes I'd jump around her, singing and dancing, just to make her laugh, but she wouldn't budge. Instead she'd turn away from me.

One day, over chocolate soy pudding, I told my mom about it. She explained that because of her dad, Mary might be suffering from abandonment issues, making it harder for her to trust people and to let them get close to her. I had no clue what Mom meant.

Coby had another explanation. He said, "That girl's in a middle-school funk. When my sister gets like that, I give her some space." Those were words I could understand.

But I didn't want to give Mary space. Not today. I wanted to hear what she thought of my fall. I sighed real loud, in an I'm-here-and-I'm-waiting-for-you kind of way. I got no response. But the little girl next to me said, "Look. Santa gave me Astro Boy boots."

"Nice," I said. "I like them."

"I have the Astro Boy movie, too. I've seen it about twenty hundred times," she said.

"You've got a real thing for him, huh?"

"Yeah. I want to marry him, but I can't yet."

"Why not? Because you're only, like, six?"

"Age is not the problem. I have to learn Japanese first. That's what he speaks, you know. The movie was dubbed."

"All righty," I said.

Finally Mary turned around.

"It was kind of dumb of you, don't you think?" she asked.

I felt my eyebrows shoot up to the top of my forehead.

"Huh?" I asked.

"You could've broken your neck, and then you'd be in a wheelchair for the rest of your life, and you'd have to sit up at the front of the classroom, where your head would always be in the way of the chalkboard, and it would be almost impossible to march in the band and to play the trumpet at the same time. Plus, it would be difficult to dance."

I hadn't thought of any of those possibilities. "Well, I'll never make band, anyway. You said I sound like a dying cat when I play. And I've never been able to dance. But, yeah, I would hate it if my head got in the way of people's view of the chalkboard."

"Exactly," Mary said. Then she sighed, like she'd just gotten a big load off her chest.

"So, are you saying that my exploit did not astound you?" I asked.

"You used the dictionary."

"No, I did not." I didn't lie. I'd used a thesaurus.

Mary turned back around and faced the window. I leaned over Astro Boy's future wife, so I could see the side of Mary's face. I could tell she wasn't really looking at anything, because her eyeballs were still. When she looks at things that are passing by, her eyes dart back and forth. Maybe everyone's do. I've only noticed it with Mary.

The bus stopped, and a bunch of kids got on. Glenna Sweet, an eighth grader, rubbed the top of my head when she went by. "What's up, Fer?" she asked, and smiled at me. I was totally taken by surprise. I'd been smacked on the backside of my head before, but no girl—except for my mom—had ever messed up my hair like that.

"Hmph," Mary retorted.

We pulled up in front of the elementary school, and I slid to the side to let the little girl out. *"Sayonara,"* she said. "That means 'good-bye' in Japanese."

"Sayonara," I said back.

A fourth grader wearing a short-sleeve shirt and no jacket held up the bus line when he stopped in front of me and yelled at the kid behind him. "Gimme a pen," he ordered. The kid scrounged through his backpack, pulled out a Sharpie, and handed it to the tough kid. "Sign my arm," he said, and handed me the pen.

"But it'll take forever to wash off," I said. "Your mom will—"

"Just your initials, then. Come on, I haven't got all day," he said.

Dang, little kids can be pushy nowadays. I scribbled my initials onto his forearm, and he nodded his approval. "Cool," he said, and headed down the aisle and off the bus without so much as a thanks.

Minutes later the bus pulled up in front of the middle school. Mom had told me that when Mary was doing her emotional thing, I should be patient. So I was being patient. I stayed in my seat and waited for her to say something.

She shoved her science book into her backpack. "The whole town is talking about you like you're some kind of living legend."

"Yeah, I know." I leaned in close, in case she wanted to say something sweet to me that she didn't want anyone else to hear.

But nothing sweet came out of her mouth. She put her hand on her forehead and said, "See what happens when you let your mind wander all the time? A brain is like a muscle, and you're losing control of yours."

I considered this, but only for a moment because there wasn't time. We were the last ones on the bus. "So, then . . . you're saying I'm not legendary?"

"Ferrell, you are a victim of circumstances. That's all." She stood up in the aisle and looked down at me. "You're getting all this attention as if you're a hero. What's heroic about a guy almost killing himself?"

"Well, yeah," I agreed. "Becoming a human avalanche and then living to tell about it isn't exactly like scoring a winning touchdown, but I guess some people think it counts for something."

"Those people are imbeciles," she said.

I stood up next to her and tucked my lunch bag under my arm. "Look, is this all because you're mad at not winning? You did great. I bet next year, if you try again and get that plug in tighter, the trophy is yours."

"No, it's not that. I mean, yeah, I wanted to win and I'd planned on winning. . . . But, no, this is about you and how you looked like you were dead. And I'd hate you forever if you died."

Her face turned bright red, and then she turned and marched toward the front of the bus. Mary Vittles had said something almost nice to me, and now she was embarrassed.

"But you would've hated me more if my head were always getting in the way of the chalkboard!" I shouted.

"Definitely," she called over her shoulder.

And there it was. No further explanation necessary.

Chapter Four

WHILE WE WERE IN MR. COMFY'S HOMEROOM, THE principal, Ms. Goodkind, made an announcement. "I expect that whoever stole the door off the third stall in the boys' bathroom will return it and properly reattach it . . . immediately."

Of course, Ms. Goodkind knew, just like the rest of us, that it was grody Brody Flushenstein who'd swiped the door, because we'd all seen him sliding down Golden Hill on it last week at the race. Ms. Goodkind could've made a big deal out of it and yelled at grody Brody over the PA system, but she didn't. I put my chin on my hand and stared out the window, thinking how principals like Ms. Goodkind should win some sort of award for not getting on kids' cases all the time.

Just then I felt a smack on the back of my head that knocked my chin out of my hand.

"Hey, man, you better go!" Eilio leaned across the aisle.

"What the . . . ? Go where?" I asked, wondering if I should smack him back.

"Ms. Goodkind just called you to the office. You didn't hear that? Get the wax cleaned out of your ears!"

I knew by the way everyone was staring at me that Eilio wasn't joking. I made my way to the main office, shuffling my feet on the linoleum in the hall. So what if I didn't hear Ms. Goodkind call for me over the loudspeaker. My ears are not plugged up. It's just that the volume of my daydreams is too loud.

I stopped at the school secretary's desk to ask if I could walk right into Ms. Goodkind's office or if I needed to knock.

"Good morning, Mr. Savage," Ms. Bland, the secretary, whispered. She stood up and reached across her desk. She gently touched my shoulder and asked, "How are you feeling? Do you think you should be in school today?"

"Yeah?" I didn't mean for it to sound like a question, but I was confused.

"I heard you came this closé to crossing over into the other world." She held her index finger close to her thumb, showing me exactly how close "this close" was.

"You mean dying?" I asked.

She gasped and then put her hand to her mouth, like I'd just said a bad word. Then she nodded.

"Well, I'm not sure how close I really came to death. I've never died before," I said.

"Was there a bright light? Did you see your dead relatives? Did they call to you?"

I thought for a moment. "No dead relatives. But the sun totally got in my eyes. I should've worn goggles."

"Oh, yes. Goggles," the secretary said slowly.

The principal's door opened, and Ms. Goodkind stepped out.

"Good morning, Ferrell," she said. "Please come in and have a seat."

I sat in the soft chair across from her desk, a chair I assumed was reserved for important people, like superintendents and angry parents. In a corner of the room a small microwave oven went *ping*. Ms. Goodkind opened the oven's door and pulled out two plates of biscuits with something in their middles. Spicy warm smells of something I'd never eaten before wafted through the room. She set one of the plates near the edge of her desk, toward me.

"Well, I'm sure your mother fed you well this morning, but I'm hoping you still have room for a celebratory breakfast. May I pour you some orange juice?" she asked.

"Sure," I said, eyeing the biscuit. Sausage. And cheese. That's what was inside it.

"I want to congratulate you on winning the sled race, Ferrell. Your victory was a miracle," she said.

"But I didn't win," I said. Gooey orange cheese and grease from the sausage dripped out onto the sides of the plates. I sucked up all the spit in my mouth and swallowed hard to keep from drooling down my chin. I wanted that cheese and sausage bad.

"Well, in the eyes of all of us here at Garfield Middle School, you're a winner. And a hero. And, oh, for goodness' sake, please, eat. Don't wait for me."

"It's not vegan by any chance, is it?" I asked. But I could tell by the way my stomach was howling, like a werewolf at the moon, the sausage was made from real meat.

"They're beef, made without any added by-products and no sulfites. I read the box before I tossed it into the recycling bin."

The back of my neck was tingling, and the hairs on my arms were standing straight up. I sat on my hands to keep from grabbing the biscuit off the plate. "I don't eat meat. No animal products. My mom forbids me to ever touch the stuff. Ever," I said. Luckily, I've had to say that exact speech enough times that I can do it automatically, without thinking.

"Oh, I'm so sorry. I didn't know. Why, the mere idea of eating animal flesh must be terribly offensive to a vegan," she said. She stood up, grabbed the plate, and dumped my biscuit right into the garbage can. She slammed down the lid. Then she took her own sausage biscuit and shoved it into her top desk drawer.

I hooked my feet around the chair's legs to keep myself from jumping up and diving headfirst into the dirty bin for cheesy sausage. This had happened to me before in the school cafeteria, when they were serving fried chicken one day. The smell was so delicious, I had to go out onto the playground for fear my hands were going to get all hairy and I was going to grow a beard and do something crazy and out of control. It took eight Oreo cookies and two boxes of

Cracker Jacks to calm me down that day.

"I wonder if your healthy eating habits might be the explanation for your amazing resilience," she mused. "You must eat a lot of vegetables."

"Almost never. I hate vegetables," I said. "We're definitely not into the health thing."

"Oh, I see. Well, then, you must be very conscious of our planet and your carbon footprint," she said.

I was glad she came up with a reason that was satisfying to her, because I didn't have one to offer her. I didn't know why we never ate meat. My parents didn't think people who did were bad people or anything, and it wasn't like they ever carried around signs saying SAVE THE COWS. Once, I asked them about it, and my mom got uncomfortable. They simply said it was too risky for us Savages and left it at that.

"Now, I'd like to request a small favor," Ms. Goodkind said. She poured a little more orange juice into my cup, and I took a big swig. I held the pulp on my tongue and felt the hairs on my arms start to relax. "My son Jeffrey was wondering if he could bring you to his first grade's show-and-tell." She looked at her watch. "It starts in fifteen minutes."

"Wow," I said. "I've never been anyone's show-and-tell before."

J. Duddy Gill

She stood up and smiled. "So, you'll do it?"

"Sure, I guess."

"Would it be too much trouble if we swing by your house and get the sled, too? I'm sure the children would love to see it. We won't let them touch it, of course," she said.

"The sled's gone. I haven't seen it since I wrecked it on the hill."

"Oh, my goodness. Yes, I remember reading in the newspaper that someone saw it blow away, like sparkling fairy dust in the wind."

"I hadn't heard that one," I said.

She held the door open for me. "What a shame it couldn't have been bronzed and put on display in our library. Imagine what that would do for our enrollment here at Garfield."

When we left Ms. Goodkind's office, Ms. Bland was writing stuff down and talking to a kid I'd never seen before.

"Ms. Goodkind," Ms. Bland said, "we'll need you to sign here in order to complete this boy's enrollment. His name is Bruce Littledood, and he's been dropped off by his dad—"

"I'm sorry, young man, but I'm not available at the moment, and I'm in a bit of a hurry." Ms. Goodkind spoke rapidly. She whispered to Ms. Bland, "Perhaps you can offer him the sausage biscuit in my top drawer. Tell him to chew slowly, and hopefully, I will be back before he finishes." Then she put her arm across my shoulders and said, "Come on, Ferrell, dear."

I looked around and caught a glimpse of a short kid wearing a plaid shirt. It was the kid with the fancy sled from the Big Sled Race, the kid who'd gotten all excited about my pollypry feather.

I waved to him and said, "Go, Broncos." Just a friendly little reminder to never accuse me of being a Packers fan.

But he scowled at me and raised up his fist. Then, without making a noise, he mouthed something that looked like *I'm going to get you.*

Chapter Five

ON OUR WAY HOME FROM THE BUS STOP, I TOLD Mary about how the plaid kid from the race was now a new kid at school. Neither of us remembered seeing him come down the hill, which wasn't really surprising. After all, as Mary says, I'm the king of daydreaming, and she'd spent some time fuming after her drain had become unplugged.

"I talked to him at the top of the hill before the race. We discussed aerodynamics. What's his name again?" Mary asked.

"Bruce something-or-other . . . Peeweeman, I think. Or Littledude—yeah. That's it. Bruce

Littledood." I stood in front of her on the sidewalk and said, "What does it look like I'm saying when I do this?" And I mouthed the words, *I'm going to get you.*

She blinked her eyes. "Do it again," she said. And I did. "It looked like you said, 'A burrito, achoo.'"

"No, that wasn't what he said. It makes no sense. Here, look at me again, and I'll say it slower."

I stood in front of Mary again, put my hands on her shoulders, and mouthed the words slowly.

"This is an invalid experiment, Ferrell. To test the results accurately, you needed to get him on tape saying whatever it was he said. There's a safety camera behind Ms. Bland's desk, and it tapes everyone who comes in. Maybe we can get access to that footage."

"Too much trouble," I argued. "This is easier. Just tell me what you think I said."

Mary sighed and shook her head. "You said, 'I'm. Going. To. Get. You.'"

"Yes! That's what I thought he said! I was right!"

"I *heard* you that time. You whispered it."

We started walking again.

"Well, it doesn't matter, because that really is what the kid said. I'm going to have to wear orange and blue *every* day just to prove to him my Broncos loyalty. Remind me never to wear any Packer green, okay?"

"I've never heard of such an adamant Broncos fan. He was probably annoyed because you were holding him up. I know I would've been. He needed Ms. Goodkind's signature, but because of you and your ridiculous immortality, she had to drive you to the elementary school to be her son's emergency show-and-tell specimen."

"Most people don't get punched because of that." I stopped on the sidewalk to think for a second. "Maybe he was swatting at a fruit fly."

"There are no fruit flies in winter," Mary said. "Look, Ferrell, you better get your fight face on or this kid is going to be on your back for the rest of the year."

"A fight face, huh? Do you mean like this?" I jutted my jaw forward and stuck out my bottom teeth.

Mary laughed. "You couldn't look menacing even if your life depended on it."

"Oh, yeah? What about this?" I furrowed my eyebrows and flared my nostrils.

Mary laughed harder. Sometimes, when I get on a roll, she laughs so hard that she barely makes any noise at all. She just squeaks through her nose.

"Or how about this to curdle your blood!" I jumped in front of her, making the Incredible Hulk pose, and grunted like a crazy man, saying, "A burrito, achoo!"

"You don't look scary, you look like Curious George!" she managed to gasp.

"Bwa-ha-ha-ha! I am the Incredibly Curious Hulk, and I shall eat the girl in the teal-blue hat!" I stomped in circles around her, like a monster-monkey, scratching my armpit until, at last, there it was: the squeaky nose thing. My mission was accomplished.

When we reached my house, Mary was still breathless from laughing, but she suddenly jolted to a stop. I looked toward where she was gazing. The pollypry feather was taped to the front door with a note attached to it.

Mary pulled off the paper and opened it. It read:

YOU'RE NOT GOING TO GET
AWAY WITH THIS.
—B. L.

Chapter Six

THE NEXT MORNING I SAT EATING MY BREAKFAST at the table with Dad while he worked on the book-shelvers' schedules for the library.

"So, what were you and Mary discussing yesterday afternoon that had you all so serious?" he asked.

"This note," I said. "We found it taped to the door." I told him about Bruce Littledood and how he'd raised his fist at me.

Mom set a plate of Fakin' Bacon in front of me and took the note from my hand. "Oh, Ferrell, for heaven's sake. What in the world could he possibly think you've gotten away with?" I dodged my head just before she was able to ruffle my hair.

"He seems to think I'm getting away with root-ing for the wrong team. For some reason he doubts my loyalty to the Broncos," I said, pointing out that today I was wearing my Peyton Manning jersey.

"People around here *do* get a little carried away about football," Mom said.

Dad looked up from his schedules. "Did you do or say something to antagonize him?"

"I barely know him. I just met him at the race. He seemed fine that day, a little scatterbrained maybe, but not psycho or anything."

"We can try to talk to his parents. But until then, if he gives you any problems, don't hesitate to use your cell phone. That's why we gave it to you."

"No way. You can't talk to his parents about this. Everyone will hear about it. Besides, Dad . . . Seriously, the kid is this big." I held my hand about a foot from the floor. "There's nothing to worry about."

"Is he a friend of Mary's?" Mom asked.

"She said she met him at the sled race." I took a swig of juice.

Mom raised her eyebrows. "And?"

"And what?" I wiped my mouth with the back of my hand. "They talked about aerodynamics."

"Aha." Mom winked at Dad. "I see what's going on here." She chuckled and went back to the kitchen sink, where she always ate her toast.

"You think maybe the boy is jealous?" Dad asked me.

"Jealous of what? The Pollypry?"

A plate crashed into the sink.

"What?" Mom whirled around and looked at Dad. "Did he say 'Polly Pry'?"

Dad's mouth dropped open.

I pulled out the feather from my backpack, and Mom put her hand over her mouth to stifle a scream. From behind her hand she squeaked out, "How did that thing make its way back into my house?"

"It's not dirty, Mom. If it had any diseases, I would have gotten one by now. Look how white it is—well, except for down here where it's all black— but pollypries must be very clean birds. "

Dad leaned over, put his hand on my arm, and spoke as if he were forcing himself to be calm. "Polly Pry is the name of a person, not a bird."

"She had feathers?" I asked.

"What you're holding in your hand, actually, is a quill pen she used in the late 1800s."

I stared at the feather, wondering what was so

scary about it. Then I looked at my dad, waiting for more of an explanation.

He pointed to the dirty end and said, "Ink. See? There used to be a metal nib."

Mom, still holding her hand to her mouth, lowered herself into a chair at the end of the table.

"Why is it so evil, Mom? The bird, er, I mean, the pen, er, no, the person . . . Polly Pry saved your uncle's life, right?"

"Exactly. My great-great-uncle Alferd was a beast."

Dad stood up, walked around the table, and put his hands on her shoulders. "It's okay, Katherine. It's history. Everyone's forgotten about it, and it has nothing to do with who you and Ferrell are now," Dad reassured her.

But Mom brushed away his arms and stood up. "I need more coffee," she said. But instead of pouring herself another cup, she got Buddy's leash, hooked it to his collar, and scooped him into her arms. "Come on, sweet boy." She kissed the top of his head and walked out the door.

Dad and I kept our eyes on the door for a long time after it slammed shut, and as soon as I was sure she was not coming right back, I turned to Dad and said, "So, how did Polly Pry save my great-great-great-uncle's life?"

Dad took a long sip of his coffee and then resituated himself in his chair. "Where do I begin . . . ," he said, and took a slow, deep breath. I happen to know librarians live to answer questions like this.

"Polly Pry . . . She was a smart, sassy woman. She was known as a sob sister, which is what they used to call women journalists who wrote stories for the paper about events that were full of gossip, and her stories were sometimes"—Dad patted his heart—"touching."

"Cut to the chase, Dad. I'm going to be late for school," I urged.

"Well, your great-great-great-uncle Alferd was in prison serving a life sentence when Polly Pry got wind of the story. She was the only one who believed the man was innocent, and she wanted to see him freed. So she wrote articles about him for the *Denver Post*. Her words were so persuasive that soon a lot of folks became interested, including the governor at that time. . . . Oh, what was his name . . . ?" Dad tapped his head.

"It doesn't matter, just keep going!"

"Let's see, it was 1901 . . . Thomas! That's who

it was. Governor Charles S. Thomas. Polly Pry must have been some good writer to convince the governor to let that man free after what he did. . . ."

I heard Mom at the front door, stomping off the snow from her boots, and Dad suddenly sat straight up in his chair. "I'll have to finish this story later, Ferrell."

"Hurry, just tell me, what did my uncle do? Was he a thief? A serial killer? A vampire?"

"Worse. What he did was taboo."

Chapter Seven

WORDS LIKE "TABOO" ARE CONFUSING TO ME.
It sounds like it would be something good. Cute, even.
Like the name of a Chihuahua or a colorful lollipop.
But it's not cute. It means doing something that is
completely and socially unacceptable. In Mr. Comfy's
homeroom I sat at my desk and tried to solve a puzzle.
The puzzle was this: Animals are considered beasts.
But Mom referred to our dog as sweet and lovely and
said her great-great-uncle was a beast. Could the man
have been more beastly than a beagle who slobbers
out the car window, attacks the mailman, and licks
himself directly underneath his tail? I had a feeling that

whatever taboo my great-great-great-uncle had committed, it was something much worse than a fart under the dinner table.

I was rudely snapped from my thoughts when Coby reached across the aisle and jabbed me in the shoulder. Bruce Littledood was being introduced to the class, and I hadn't even noticed. I tried to tune in to what was going on.

"And until now he's been homeschooled by his father, who is a history professor at the university . . . ," Mr. Comfy was saying.

Standing in front of the class, the little dude looked completely harmless.

"So what made you decide to join us here at Garfield Middle School?" Mr. Comfy asked.

Bruce shrugged. "I don't know," he said. "I had been helping my dad with a big historical research project, and when we finished, I felt like I needed a break."

"Well," Mr. Comfy said, laughing. "I do hope we can keep things interesting here for you, since, ahem, I'd never thought of going to a traditional school as being a break."

"Oh, it is"—Bruce Littledood laced his fingers together, pushed the palms of his hands right toward me, and popped every knuckle—*padadadadada-dow*—"a break."

"I have something I'd like to share with the class," Littledood continued. Mr. Comfy watched as Littledood stepped out of the room and returned with a big trophy in his arms. It was the Big Sled Race on Golden Hill trophy. He used both hands to raise it over his head, and then he smiled like he was about to get his photo taken.

The class muttered a few comments, like, "I was wondering who won" and "Oh, nice" and "Huh, that was, like, over a week ago."

And then someone said, "Did you see Savage? Man, that was one freakin' scary fall!"

"Yeah, Savage, you're a ninja Gumby!"

"It was epic!"

"He was like that Bugs Bunny cartoon when Bugs gets rolled up into a giant snowball, and all you see are his feet and the tops of his ears."

"No way!" I said. "You couldn't see my ears."

The class went into an uproar, and a few kids left their seats to pat me on the back. Littledood lowered his trophy and glared at me.

Mr. Comfy called us to order. When everyone was quiet and back in their seats, he said, "Bruce, you said you have something to announce?"

"Yes. I'm offering a rematch, next Saturday, to any-one who prefers a more challenging, death-defying sled race. It will be held on Specter Slope. If you think you can survive, you're invited to participate." He cradled his trophy in his arms and looked right at me. "There's a sign-up sheet outside the cafeteria."

He stuck his tongue into his cheek, as if he were cleaning peanut butter out of his gums, and took the empty seat right in the front of the class.

Another sled race. No, thanks. The thought of it made me want to put my head down on my desk and take a nap.

In the cafeteria at lunch, I sat at our usual table. Coby plopped down next to me, and Eilio and the other guys slid their trays onto the round table.

"So, that's the kid who tried to beat you up in the office yesterday?" Coby asked.

I nodded.

"Gotta watch out for those shrimpy guys. Sometimes they're the meanest and the strongest," Eilio added.

"Yeah." Grody Brody Flushenstein stuffed his mouth with a peanut butter sandwich. "You're gonna be sorry you ever made him mad."

"But I didn't do anything to him. He has no reason to be mad," I protested. I pulled the thermos from my lunch box, opened it, and looked inside. Beans and rice again. I put the lid back on and reached into the front pocket of my jeans to fish out a bag of Skittles and two boxes of extra-sour Cry Babies.

"He's in the hallway right now trying to solicit kids to race on Specter Slope," Eilio said.

"How many signed up so far?" grody Brody asked.

"Zero," Eilio said.

I half listened as I sorted through a handful of Skittles. Orange ones were my favorites. Sometimes I matched them with a yellow for an extra-tart flavor.

"Who would want to race down Specter Slope? It's not even a sledding hill," Coby said.

"Besides, it's time to move on. The big race is over. He won, and he carries that trophy around like it's his girlfriend," Eilio said.

I looked up. "Since when do guys carry their girlfriends around?"

Eilio punched me in the arm. "Very funny! You know what I meant."

"I think he's got it in for you, Savage," grody Brody said.

"I know that. But why?" I asked.

"It doesn't matter," grody Brody answered.

"Brody's right. He wants to take you down, and you're going to have to stand up to him," Coby said.

"Oooh, whatcha gonna do to scare him, Ferrie?" Eilio asked in a high-pitched voice.

"I don't want to scare him. I don't have time." While the guys were talking nonsense, I licked my lips and rubbed a green Skittle across them, painting my lips green with the candy coating. I smiled big at my friends, and they cracked up.

There was a tap on my shoulder. Mary looked down at me, ready to say something, but when she saw my green lips, she just shook her head and said, "Why do I bother?"

I licked my mouth furiously and wiped it with the back of my hand. "Wait!" I said as she walked away. I slid out of my seat and went after her. "You should bother because . . . you just should. Bother with what?"

She turned to face me. "You missed the corners," she said.

I rubbed the corners of my mouth until they were sore.

"Clean now?" I asked.

She ignored the question. "Bruce Littledood says he has a proposition for you," she said.

"A proposition?"

"It's like a deal."

"I know what a proposition is." I rubbed the corners of my mouth again, just to be sure the green was gone.

"I told him we'd meet him at the fountain in the park after school. He wants me there too, because he says he knows you and I have been keeping a secret."

Was I supposed to know what the secret was? Asking would only make me look dumb. So I said "All righty" and popped a Skittle into my mouth.

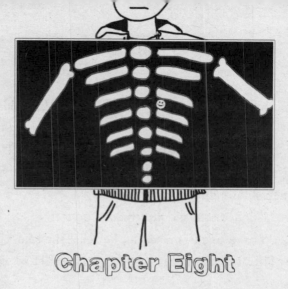

Chapter Eight

MARY'S BOOT HEELS DRAGGED ON THE DRY SIDE-walk as we walked to the park. There were patches of snow in the shady places under the trees and along the northern edges of the houses, but Colorado was doing its faux sunny springtime-in-the-winter thing. I took off my hoodie and shoved it into my backpack.

It's funny how when you say certain words, you see them in your head, too. It was going to take some effort to remember that the kid's name is Littledood and not Little Dude, especially since I'd already gotten into the habit of seeing him as a little dude.

"You know, your name would be completely different

if you spelled it *M-E-R-R-Y* instead of *M-A-R-Y*," I said.

"Merry Vittles? Are you kidding me? That could be the title of a cookbook," she said. She walked faster, and her heels sounded like they might dig trenches through the concrete.

I laughed, but she just trudged on.

"You're one to make fun, Ferrell," she said.

I had to run and catch up to hear her. "How so?" I asked.

"*F-E-R-A-L*," she spelled, breathless from walking so fast.

"So?"

"So, don't you know what it means to be feral?"

I thought it meant that a person couldn't have babies, but, luckily, she didn't give me time to answer—because, wow, that was way wrong. She continued, "It means 'undomesticated.' 'Untamed.' Like those wild cats living in our alley that look like house cats. They eat fly-covered garbage from the Dumpsters."

"Mmm, I bet their breath smells good. How's mine?" I ran in front of her to blow in her face, but before I had a chance to breathe on her, she got up in my face instead. Her nose was, like, three inches away from mine, and she reached out and squeezed

my arms, holding me there for what seemed like forever.

"Stop it!" she said to me.

"Stop what?" I asked. All I could think was, *Hey,
look how close her mouth is to mine.* Her breath
went straight out of her lungs and right up my nose
and into my lungs. We were connected by a warm
stream of air.

"You're acting like you don't even care. In a
matter of minutes you are going to confront a boy
who feels hostile toward you, probably because you
provoked him somehow, and he might be about to
pummel you to smithereens." Then she pushed me
away, and I stumbled into the grass.

I knew I should've responded, but the truth was,
I'd hardly heard a word she had just said. When her
face was so close to mine, that yellow marble with
the kissy face, the one that was lodged just below my
heart and right above my stomach, was tickling me,
and I had to gather up all my concentration to keep
from laughing like a big doofus.

As I got back my balance, I tried to replay what
she'd just said. We had reached the corner of the
park, and we walked toward the big fountain. I managed to settle my insides but still couldn't quite talk.

Finally, I broke the silence. "Nobody's going to pummel me," I said.

"How do you know?" Now she sounded worried.

"Because I'm not going to let them."

"How will you stop them?" she asked.

"I'll run. I'll climb a tree. I'll stand behind you." I smiled at her when I said this, but she wasn't in the mood to laugh. "I'll tell him to knock it off."

"How brave," she said.

We had reached the fountain.

"What could the guy possibly want?" I asked.

"Jeez, Ferrell, do I have to spell everything out for you? Has it never occurred to you that maybe, just maybe, he likes me, and since you and I hang out together so much, he thinks our secret is that we're a couple, and maybe, just maybe, he wants to fight you?"

"No," I said.

"Didn't you see how he looked right at me when Mr. Comfy was introducing him to the class?"

"I missed it," I replied.

"Figures. You miss everything that's important. It was when he was bragging about how he's so good at history and that researching family trees is his specialty."

Family trees? Yawn. Well, no wonder I hadn't heard him.

"So he's good at history." I pretended to snore, like just thinking about history would bore me to sleep. "Poor guy. I guess he's gotta have something to impress the girls," I said. "And were you impressed?"

I didn't breathe while I waited for her to answer.

"He said he knows how to find access to anyone's past, and their relatives, too."

"Nice." I rolled my eyes. "Wouldn't a fortune-teller be more useful?"

"Stop talking like you think I'm ridiculous. And for just a moment try to imagine that there might be someone who thinks I'm something more than a spell-check."

Oh, she was more than a spell-check. And, oh yes, I could imagine he liked her.

"You didn't answer my question," I said. "Did he impress you?"

She shrugged one shoulder. That meant that the other shoulder was probably impressed a whole lot. I wondered if he used big words.

Before I knew what was happening, both my hands balled into fists.

Chapter Nine

BRUCE LITTLEDOOD LOOKED LIKE THE KIND OF kid who'd grow up and have a big, hairy mustache hanging over his lip. He stood on the ledge of the fountain, towering over Mary and me, wearing khaki pants, a plaid shirt under his unzipped jacket, and brown shoes.

"I'm pleased you decided to meet me here," he said.

I tugged at my jersey. "Go, Broncos!" I said.

Littledood acted like he didn't hear me. That's just the kind of thing a guy with a mustache would do.

"Hello, Mary." He smiled. "How are you today?"

"Look," I interrupted, "Mary doesn't even like mustaches. Can you please just tell us why we're here?" The glare of the sun behind his head made my eyes water.

"Who said anything about mustaches?" Mary asked.

"Never mind," I answered.

Littledood turned to me. "Do you recall our first encounter?"

"Of course I remember. I met you at the Big Sled Race, and we had a friendly little chat. The next time I saw you, you either made a fist at me or you caught a fruit fly. I'm still willing to give you the benefit of the doubt."

"Indeed, it was a fist," he said. "Now would you like me to tell you why?"

I took a deep breath to prepare myself for the moment. I was sure he was about to confess his love for Mary and then beat me up because he thought I was a threat to his possible relationship with Mary. And maybe I was a threat. Maybe I was!

"I'm waiting," Littledood prompted.

I would do whatever I had to do, but it was hard to feel tough with Littledood towering over me on the fountain's edge the way he was. So I said, "You know, before you tell me, would you mind stepping down from up there? If I face the sun for too long, I'm likely to get a burn and, you know, skin cancer and all that."

He hopped down to eye level—oops, no, more like his eyes to my shoulder level.

"What do you want to tell us?" I asked.

He cleared his throat and composed himself. I wondered if maybe he had a speech planned and I had messed it all up. "Well," he began, making his voice go deep. "Allow me to ask you a question. Before today, did you know I won the Big Sled Race on Golden Hill?"

I shook my head and then looked at Mary.

"No," she said.

"We all just kind of figured no one won," I said.

"Does that not sound absurd to you?" Littledood demanded, his eyes flashing with anger. "Of course, in any kind of competition, there is always a winner. After all, a winner is the one who finishes fastest, and with the exception of a tie, there is always someone who finishes faster than the others. Hence the word 'race.'"

Oh yeah, there was no doubt in my mind that the little dude had written all this down and had practiced it before reciting it to Mary and me. I mean, what kid besides Mary says "hence," unless he prepared in advance?

Unless he used "hence" to impress Mary.

I needed to get her out of there before he started throwing around the really big words. "Well, you won. That's awesome. Congratulations," I said. Let's wrap it up here.

"I don't remember seeing you come down on your . . . ," Mary said. "What did you call it again?"

"The Titanium Blade Runner," I answered.

Littledood tossed his head. "It is an amazing sled."

"How arrogant," Mary said.

Yay! That'll teach him to keep his hences to himself. She obviously didn't like him. He knew it, I knew it, and we could all go home now. I put my hand on my stomach and realized I was starving.

"Again, congratulations. Sorry I missed your big moment," I repeated. A yummy vision of the snacky kind appeared in my brain. A banana, perfectly ripe, smothered with peanut butter, rolled in carob chips, and topped with powdered sugar. And on top of that—

I turned to leave, but Mary didn't budge.

"Yes, everyone should be sorry," Littledood said.

"Mr. Spinelli said my time broke the record for the race. Nobody in thirty years has gone down Golden Hill faster than me on my Titanium Blade Runner."

"If it was such a big deal, how did we miss it?" Mary asked.

"I'll tell you how. Do you remember how many entrants there were in the race?" Littledood's eyes darted back and forth from Mary to me.

I shrugged.

"Sixty," Mary said.

"And what number were you?" he asked me.

I thought hard and tried to remember what number had been on the card Mr. Spinelli had pinned to my jacket.

"Fifty-nine," Mary supplied.

"I was the only person to go after you, Ferrell Savage. But you stopped the show. You were literally carried away by the crowd, and all that was left was me and Mr. Spinelli."

"Aw, that totally stinks!" I said. "Seriously, you should complain about that. In fact, if you want to call Mr. Spinelli from my house, we could go right now. Do you like bananas and—"

"I don't want to complain to Mr. Spinelli. I want a rematch."

"Right. Well, good luck with that. I hope you win again."

"I can't win. No one signed up for it. Have a look." He pulled the sign-up sheet from his pocket and unfolded it. On the lines where kids were sup- posed to write their names, it said:

Been there, done that, it stank

Not on that stupid slope

See ya next year

Srsly?

"Gosh," I said. "I can't say I blame them. Golden Hill's sled race is about the tradition and the crowd. It's something to do on the day after Christmas, not on a Saturday in January."

"It makes no difference to me that they won't be racing. You're the only contestant I care to beat. You were recognized as a hero, but I have the better, faster sled," Bruce said.

"Well, I don't want to race again," I said. "Besides, I don't have my Pollypry anymore. It disappeared."

"It's in my garage. If you agree to compete, you shall have it back."

"You've had it in your garage all this time?" Weird. And even though Coby and Eilio had said I could've auctioned it off on eBay and made tons of money, I honestly didn't care if I never saw the Pollypry again. I looked at Mary, wondering if she would be impressed if I agreed.

"Better luck next year, Bruce," she said.

Oh, thank you, Mary Vittles. I was off the hook!

Mary and I were both turning toward home and snacks when Bruce said, "Not so fast. If you don't agree to a rematch, I'll let everyone know your and Mary's dirty, little secret."

"What secret?" Mary asked.

"And what's so dirty and little about it?" I wanted to know.

"You were either brave or stupid to name your sled after Polly Pry and then to admit that your uncle was the one she saved."

"I'm not stupid! I didn't know Polly Pry was a person. I thought it was a bird." Okay, that sounded stupid.

"But certainly you know about your ancestors, don't you?"

"Uh, actually, I don't," I said. "But it's history. Who cares?"

"It's family history. And family history is everything! It's who you are!" Littledood yelled and waved his arms in the air. A lady walking her dog stopped to stare.

"You're wrong, Littledood. We are not made of our family histories!" Mary yelled back.

Littledood shook his head, as if he were getting water out of his ears. "Oh my gosh! I get it now. Your own secret has been kept from you as well. You all don't even know!" He laughed wickedly.

Some people are intrigued by drama and secrecy, but me, I get bored. I really wished he'd get to the point.

"I'll give you until Monday to find out what it is, and then you can, one"—he held up one finger—"let me humiliate you by telling everyone in school. Or, two"—he held up a second finger (I knew he would)—"you can take me up on my challenge and give me the opportunity to show Golden Hill what a real hero looks like, and I'll keep your secret safe right here"—and he patted his chest with his free hand, and then held up a third finger (this guy was so predictable)—"or, three . . . Well, there is no number three. You have just two choices."

Chapter Ten

I SPOONED PEANUT BUTTER ONTO THE SECOND half of my third banana, bit into it, and set it on a plate. My stomach was finally getting full. I took a big swig of cherry Kool-Aid to wash everything down.

Mary was pacing back and forth, looking out the front window for Mom, who had taken the laptop to the coffee shop to work on a book she'd been writing.

"Don't worry. As soon as she gets here we'll look it up," I said. "We've got till Monday."

Mary flung herself onto the couch and hid her face in her hands. I sat down next to her. "You know," I said, "that kid would make an awesome actor. He'd be great in one of those movies where people just talk and nothing happens. Seriously—with the mysterious and threatening note, the way he eyeballed me, the whole gig? Beautifully done, if you ask me. I wish he'd move to Hollywood."

"Are you trying to make me feel better?" Mary asked without looking up. "Because you're not."

"Feel better about what?" I wondered. Mary sure could confuse the bejeebers out of me.

"He obviously doesn't like me, and after I told you I thought he was going to fight you . . . over me . . . I feel imprudent and silly," she said, still hiding her face.

Maybe this was one of those middle-school funk episodes Coby had told me about. I took a deep breath and dove into Mary's pool of angst.

"No way. You could never be an imprude. Besides," I said, "it's not like anyone will ever find out. The mighty little dude doesn't know we thought he was in love with you, right? And you didn't tell anyone else."

"No." She lifted her face from her hands. "But, still, I looked like an idiot in front of you."

"You've looked like an idiot in front of me before. Tons of times. So don't worry," I reassured her. "And I'll never tell anyone you thought the little dude had a thing for you." I felt my chest tighten around the marble and was almost too afraid to ask this important question. "What about you? Do you have a thing for him?"

She squeezed up her face the same way she did the time I accidentally made her lemonade with salt instead of sugar.

Phew.

We sat quietly for a minute, and finally Mary looked at the clock on the wall and sighed. "I'm exhausted," she said. "And my mom should be home by now. She catered a big lunch party at the inn, and she probably has chicken cordon bleu in boxes for our dinners." She picked up her backpack, and dragged it to the front door. "If you find anything on the Internet, call me. If not, I'll just see you tomorrow. I think I'm going to go to bed early."

"I'm sure whatever it is, it's nothing. I'm not worried," I said.

"Do you ever worry about anything?" she asked.

I thought for a minute. "I'm down to just the root beer barrels and Big League Chew in my Halloween stash, and it's only January."

"Must be nice," she said sleepily, and closed the door behind her.

Chapter Eleven

THAT EVENING MOM AND DAD WENT TO THE neighbors' house for cocktails. I sat at the kitchen table and opened the laptop. Google is always a good place to start. I typed the only clues I had: "Polly Pry" and "Alferd."

I clicked on the first Google entry, which brought me to the Hinsdale County Museum website. The article was long, and my eyes couldn't even focus on all those words that seemed to walk around the page, like scatterbrained black ants. My brain tried to make them walk a straight line, but it was hard. I back-tracked to the Google list and tried a few other sites until I found one with a short blurb about Polly Pry: "Polly Pry was the reporter for the *Denver Post* who is best remembered for her investigative reporting in the case of Alferd Packer."

Alferd Packer! So, that was the guy's name. When Littledood had asked me if I was a Packer, he hadn't meant Green Bay, he'd meant Alferd Packer.

I went back to the Google page and typed in "Alferd Packer," scrolled through until I found the shortest article, and read. My eyes darted around the page, catching words. Born in Pennsylvania . . . Served in the Civil War . . . San Juan Mountains . . . Met Chief Ouray in Montrose, Colorado . . . Snowbound in the Rocky Mountains . . .

"Argh!" I shouted into the empty house. "Get on with it! Tell me what taboo thing my great-great-great-uncle did!" Reading tortures me more than anything!

This kind of work called for my secret weapon of concentration. Skittles. I kept an emergency bag stashed behind some books on the shelf. I grabbed them and shoved a handful into my mouth.

My head felt a little clearer, and I continued reading.

"It is said Alfred Packer became known as Alferd

when a tattoo artist misspelled his name on his arm."

Useless information.

I scrolled down to the end of the page and read in the same pattern as I read a lot of homework assignments: beginning with the last sentence and ending with the first.

"He was buried at Littleton Cemetery near Denver."

I scrolled up, skipping around the paragraphs.

"He was sentenced to be hanged, but later the charge was reduced to manslaughter, and he was given forty years to be served at the prison in Cañon City."

Manslaughter! That was it! I was definitely onto something. My eyes got caught on the photo of a guy with a bushy mustache and beard. I stared into his wild, scary eyes and wondered if I was seeing something familiar. Did I look like him?

Just then there was a loud thump in the living room, and I almost screamed. It was just Buddy, who had jumped off the couch.

"Quiet, Budster. You nearly scared the Skittles out of me." He trotted to my chair. "Now I lost my place."

I scratched Buddy's chin with one hand and

put the index finger of my other hand on the word on the screen, making sure I was reading it right. "'Manslaughter.' Yep." I shivered. "My great-great-great-uncle killed people." Before scrolling down, I rubbed my hands together. I wasn't sure I wanted to know more. But I couldn't stand not knowing, either. Maybe he'd killed bad guys, like the kind who robbed and murdered people on trains.

I took a deep breath and read on.

"Blah, blah, blah." My eyes skimmed around the page, hoping key words would jump out at me. "Oh, here . . . 'Alferd Packer became known as the infamous Colorado Cannonball and may be the only cannonball to be tried in the US court system.' Huh."

I leaned back in my chair and folded my arms across my chest. A cannonball. There was a picture of Alferd Packer standing next to a bunch of other guys with bushy beards, but there was no picture of a cannon and no further explanation of what was meant by "Colorado Cannonball," at least none that jumped out at me. I could have gone to another website, but reading had exhausted me. How do people get through entire books this way? I once made it to the top of the climbing wall at the rec center, and I wasn't nearly as tired then as I was now.

Before I could go on, I needed food—something more substantial than Skittles. I slid away from the table and headed to the kitchen to heat up some left-over pasta and Tastes Just Like Chicken strips. As I loaded up my plate, I thought about the information I'd gathered and came to this conclusion: Alferd Packer was a human cannonball who was charged for manslaughter, probably because after he was shot out of a cannon, he hit some people and killed them. He'd used his body as a weapon. But, still, he couldn't have fired the cannon if he was inside it. Shouldn't the person who fired it have been the one charged for murder? It's not a cannonball's fault when it hits people and kills them. In my opinion, this did not make Mom's great-great-uncle a "beast."

But, wait, Mom's maiden name was Parker, not Packer. Close but . . . still not the same. Maybe another tattoo artist mistake?

I took my pasta to the couch and flipped on the TV. I always do my best thinking in front of the TV.

I wondered what the big deal was. Granted, I hadn't read the whole article as carefully as Mary would've, but I'd definitely gotten the gist of it. And, frankly, what did my great-great-great-uncle's being a manslaughtering human cannonball have to do with me? I hadn't killed anybody! I would never! Besides, from what I'd read, it sounded like Great-Great-Great-Uncle Alferd had been treated unfairly. Polly Pry had obviously believed he was innocent. I had no secret to be ashamed of, and Littledood could tell the world.

After my plate was scraped clean, I leaned my head back into the sofa and was just dozing off when I heard Mom scream from the dining room.

"What's wrong?" I yelled. I flew off the couch and ran in to see.

Mom stood at the table, staring at the screen and holding her hand over her mouth. Dad leaned over her, reading from behind her shoulder and rubbing her back to calm her.

"How did you find this? How did you know?" she asked.

"Ferrell was bound to find out someday, Katherine. Now's a good time to talk about it," Dad said. He pulled out a chair for her to sit, and she did. I ran to the sink and brought her a cup of water. She drank it and seemed to feel better. I sat in the chair across from her.

"So now you know. All right," she said to me. "I'm sure you have some questions about what this means to you. Yes, this horrible, disgusting, foul excuse for a human being is related to us. Thank goodness my grandfather changed my family's name from Packer to Parker, so no one makes the connection. As for you and me, Ferrell—and anyone else who has the Packer blood—well, all we can do is live our lives as honestly and cleanly as possible."

"All righty," I said. Honest and clean. I could do that. "I'm confused, though. Was Great-Great-Great-Uncle Alferd in a circus or what?"

Mom tilted her head. "Well, the story goes that he was offered a job as a sideshow freak in a circus, but he didn't take the job," she said.

"But what about the other times he was a cannonball? Was that his job?" I asked.

Mom and Dad both stared at me, blank-faced. There was silence as they each blinked about three or four times.

Finally, Mom spoke. "No, sweetheart. He wasn't a cannonball. He was a *cannibal*. Your great-great-great-uncle Alferd Packer killed people and then ate them."

Chapter Twelve

I AM RELATED TO A MONSTER. MOM AND I HAVE monster blood running through our systems. I had always sensed that there was something wrong with me. That if I just tasted real meat, I wouldn't be able to stop eating it. I even went through a biting phase when I was little. Mary remembers a time when I bit her arm and gave her a bruise. Now I understand. I was trying to eat her. I tossed and turned all night thinking about it, and when I gave up on sleeping, I decided to get the laptop and read the whole article more carefully, even if it took me until morning to do so. Which it did.

After learning more about him, I had some heart for the guy. I mean, I had a better understanding of how his situation had called for drastic measures.

I zoomed in on his photograph and made it bigger on the screen. Most of his face was covered by his big, bushy beard, so my eyes focused on his eyes. He didn't look hateful or mean. He looked confused. Bewildered. Maybe a little bit sad under his wide-brimmed hat.

When Mary came over on Saturday, I tried to explain it casually, as if cannibalism were a common family secret.

"Here's the dealio," I began. "My great-great-great-uncle was Alferd Packer, and he ate people." I blurted out the words. "See, he was trekking over the Rocky Mountains to look for gold with some other guys, and they got lost in a blizzard, and they didn't have any more food, so, naturally he was hungry, and, well, he ate the other five guys." Mary's eyes bulged. "He was about to die of starvation, and he was desperate. What else could he do?" Mary didn't answer. "Hey, like Dad says, it's history. Littledood can tell the world for all I care. Okay," I rambled on, "I guess it's better if no one knows—I mean, can you imagine when Eilio gets ahold of this? He'll never let me live it down. But, still, it's not worth another sled ride down any hill, and certainly not down Specter Slope."

Mary was pale. She sat down on the couch, leaned forward, and put her face in her hands. "I can't believe it," she said. "This is awful." Her voice was muffled, and she shook her head.

"Well, I think I've got it under control, though. I'm pretty sure that if I stay away from meat and other animal stuff, I won't have a problem." I tried to sound firm about it, even though I wasn't at all certain. "After all, I've never eaten anyone." I almost added "yet," but I stopped myself.

"I'm not worried about you," Mary said, her face still covered. "What are people going to think if they find out?"

"I know it's gross and all, but it was a long time ago, and who cares now? Nobody's even heard of Alferd Packer," I said.

Mary stood up and paced around the room. "Everyone in Colorado knows who Alferd Packer is!"

"Maybe smart people like you, and people who listen in history class. But not regular people like me."

Mary sighed and held up her hands in disgust. "I

can't believe this is happening to me," she said.

"But this is my problem," I said. "It has nothing to do with you."

Mary's voice trembled as she spoke. "There's something I never told you before. I've never told anyone." She sat back on the couch, and I sat next to her. "My great-great-grandfather was Shannon Wilson Bell."

"Uh-oh," I said. Now it was starting to make sense. "He was one of the guys Alferd ate."

Mary nodded.

"Gosh, I'm sorry, Mary. I always knew there was something weird about me. I guess it goes back a long way. Wow, I'm really sorry." What else could I say? What does any guy say to the girl he's crushing on when he finds out his family ate hers for dinner? This could be a real relationship buster.

"So, you come from a long line of weirdos. At least your family shows some strength and gumption. I'm related to someone who was stupid enough to be eaten by a cannibal."

"Maybe it's not because he was stupid. Maybe he was a slow runner," I pointed out.

"What kind of idiot goes up to the mountains and gets himself eaten by another person? Couldn't he have outsmarted Packer instead? No, because obviously he was a loser."

"But that's him, not you," I protested.

"It's a pattern. Don't you see? My great-great-grandfather was on his way to finding gold, but he got eaten instead. Then my great-grandfather made a fortune, lost all his money in the stock market, and jumped out the window."

"Ooh." I cringed.

"My father's great-aunt was a genius who invented a carpet cleaner that contained toxic ingredients and who went to jail when hundreds of cats and dogs got sick. And my grandfather? Well, he wrote a book that turned out to be made up of words he stole from other writers. See? Everyone from my dad's side of the family is a loser!"

"Wow, that's a lot of bad luck," I said. "What about your dad?"

"My dad was fine until he invested everything in a company that went bankrupt right when Mom found out she was pregnant with me. He lost all the money. That's when he left her."

"What's he doing now?" I asked.

"He's a telemarketer. He calls people's homes while they're eating dinner and asks them if they want to switch their cable provider." She stood up like she was about to leave, but didn't. "That's what my future looks like."

In all the years I'd known Mary, I'd never seen her look so small, like a mouse in a dark corner. She stood there, fidgeting with the tie of her hoodie and looking down at the floor.

"You're not like them," I repeated. I got up from my chair and took a step closer to her. I was surprised she didn't back up. "You're not stupid. And I don't know about your dad, but I do know he'd have to be stupid to leave you and your mom."

Then Mary did the weirdest thing I've ever known her to do. She stepped toward me and wrapped her arms around me for half a split second, maybe less. Then she pushed herself away, and I was flung in the opposite direction. And as I was being flung away, I realized what had just happened.

Mary had hugged me.

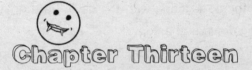

Chapter Thirteen

BEFORE DINNER MOM SENT MARY AND ME DOWN to Spinelli's for a bag of red lentils. It had snowed an inch or two the previous night, and our feet crunched as we walked. I felt a little awkward after the hug and couldn't think of anything to say. Mary was quiet too.

The way I saw it was like this: Mary's and my friendship was like my old Converse shoes. I had outgrown them in the fall, and as much as I knew I needed and wanted a new pair, I wasn't quite ready to make the move. I had worn them—with the holes in the big toe knuckles and the red paint from Mary's and my summer camp mural—for almost a year and a half. Then one day the shoes felt tight and squeezey, making all my toes aware of one another. For weeks I tried loosening the laces, wearing the shoes without socks, wearing them in the shower so they'd stretch out when they dried on my feet. But nothing worked. It was beyond my control. My feet had grown, and it was time for a new pair of shoes.

Mary's and my friendship had become squeezey, and it was time for something new.

We sat at the deli counter, drinking root beer; Mr. Spinelli's treat. "Anything for you, Miracle Survivor Boy," he had said.

I sat high on my stool and stretched my arms over my head. "Ah," I said, "I feel like the weight of last night's dark hours has been lifted off my shoulders."

"Way to mix the metaphors," she said.

"Metaphor, schmetaphor. Who cares?" I leaned forward and put my elbows on the counter.

"Now I see why the little conniver looked right at me when he talked about family trees," Mary said. "He knows I'm related to Shannon Bell."

"Yep. The kid knows his stuff all right." I took a long swig of root beer.

"I simply cannot resign myself to the fact that I'm related to such a long line of defeatists."

"Tell me about it. How do you think I felt when I found out I was related to a cannibal? But, you know, I think everything's going to be okay. I'm glad I don't have to race Littledood again." I slid to the edge of my seat, closer to Mary. "And I think it's cool . . . our little moment back at the house. You know . . . our sort-of hug thing."

"Ferrell Savage, you most certainly are going to race against Bruce Littledood, and you're going to tell him so first thing Monday morning, because I will not have people standing around, looking at me, just waiting for me to fail the same way my ancestors did. And as for a hug, well, you're just plain crazy, thinking I'd embrace someone who devours my relatives, because that was no hug. I was looking at an ad on your computer screen, and you got in the way, so I simply moved you, is all."

I was speechless. What had just happened?

"I'm impaled," I finally said.

"You mean 'appalled,'" she shot back with a snarl.

No, I meant "impaled." I felt a sharp pain right in that spot between my heart and my stomach, right where that stupid marble lived. I was pretty sure the kissy face had grown pointy teeth and had just chomped me from the inside out. I hoped to never experience that kind of impalement again for as long as I lived.

Chapter Fourteen

PEOPLE THOUGHT I WAS THE NEXT BEST THING to Superman, just because I'd survived the fall down the hill. But they were wrong. All I had done was throw together a weak contraption and then be dumb enough to enter a race with it. And dumber than that, I'd done it all for Mary. I was not proud.

From then on, no more doing anything for Mary. Mary could go fly a kite in an electrical storm during a tornado after eating a dozen donuts and get dropped in an ocean filled with pirate ships and sharks where she'd get a cramp and . . .

Never mind. I didn't really want anything bad to happen to Mary.

Anyway, Bruce Littledood was giving me a chance to redeem myself. And that's what I was going to do. I'd take my Pollypry and make it stronger than before. I'd fix it so it wouldn't swallow me up and spit me out its backside, like it did last time. I couldn't expect to win against the Titanium Blade Runner, but I could prove to myself that I was brave enough to try. When I lost, well, at least the town would have a new hero. I really was never cut out for the job.

On Sunday I planned to tell Mary that I was going to race, but she didn't show up. All day I paced around waiting for her. Was I sad that she didn't come? Did I miss her? No way. Not one bit. In fact, I started to wonder why her mother made her come over, anyway. It wasn't like she couldn't take care of herself when she was alone at her own house.

On Monday morning I started to put on my semi-new Converse and thought of Mary's and my squeezey friendship. But as I slid my feet into the shoes, I realized our relationship wasn't changing. She was just as bossy as ever. I pulled off the shoes and threw them to the back of my closet, next to my old, well-worn, and too-small Converse. I couldn't wear either pair. The last thing I wanted was to look at my feet and be reminded of Mary.

I searched the bottom of my closet and considered

my other options. I had my snow boots, but the wool lining made my feet sweat in school. That left me with my golf shoes. Dad had bought me a pair, hoping I'd take up golf with him, but it didn't happen. I kept getting distracted, and instead of hitting the ball, I'd dig up a clump of dirt next to the ball and send it flying. We quit playing because Dad was afraid that after I put so many holes in the course, the manager was going to make us pay for repairs.

I picked up the shoes. They were bright white on top, and underneath they had shiny, sharp Big Bertha Spikes, like the teeth of a shark. Perfect. Nobody was going to bother me with these on my feet.

I went downstairs, trying not to stomp and click in my shoes. Mom was in the kitchen, pouring hot water into the coffee press.

"Ferrell, honey? You don't look like your usual self this morning," she said.

"I'm not sick," I grumbled. I grabbed the orange juice from the fridge.

"No, I didn't mean that you look sick," she said. She handed me a glass for my juice, then smoothed out the back of my hair. "You're just not soft and sweet like you usually are."

I was done with soft and sweet.

"Is something going on with you? Are you all right?" she asked.

"I'm just dandy," I said, thinking "dandy" would sound cooler than it did.

"Well, all righty, then," she said. "So, what would you like for breakfast, Mr. Dandy?"

"Don't call me that," I said.

I sat down, and Mom put a box of Frosted Grainios in front of me. She shook her head and said, "Looks like someone's in a—what did Coby tell you it was?—a middle-school funk."

"Boys don't funk."

"Of course they do. Growing up is painful and difficult. You start caring about things you didn't used to care about. Grades, girls, your clothes."

"Care about my clothes? That'll never happen," I said, hiding my feet under my chair. Man, I really hoped I wasn't going to start caring about grades now too. What a time suck. And girls? I was already through with that phase, thank you very much.

"Hey, Mom? How would you feel if everyone knew we were related to Alferd Packer?"

She shuddered at the mention of his name. Then she said, "I don't care what people think or know about us. My biggest concern has been to protect you from feeling afraid. Afraid of yourself."

I wondered if she wanted to eat meat the same way I did, and maybe she was afraid she would suddenly start eating her friends and family too. "He may not have been a monster, though," I said. And then I told her what I knew was true. "You're definitely not a monster, Mom."

"Thanks, Ferrell," she said.

At school I stood at my locker, looking for my science homework, which was due in three and a half minutes and wasn't even close to finished.

"So have you told him yet?" Mary's voice came from right next to my ear, but I refused to look at her.

"I never told you I was going to race. What makes you think I am?" I snapped.

"Well, you are, aren't you?"

I hate it when she thinks she knows everything.

"Yes," I grumbled.

"Right. So when are you going to tell Littledood?"

"I could tell him right before science class if you'd just give me a chance," I said.

"What's with the shiny shoes? Are you playing golf after school?" she asked.

"As a matter of fact, I am. I won't be home."

"Even Tiger Woods can't play in the snow. Wow,

you must be really good," she noted. I could actually hear her roll her eyes.

I gritted my teeth and then started mumbling.

"You think that just because you're muttering under your breath I can't hear you," she said. "But I hear you perfectly. Something about me flying a kite into a tornado over pirate- and shark-infested waters. Am I right?"

I slammed my locker shut and looked her in the face. "Did you know Hitler was a vegetarian?" I asked.

"What's your point?"

I didn't know either. I guess I was trying to scare her by showing her I could be a powerful dictator if I wanted, but, on second thought, the last thing a middle-school kid with cannibalistic tendencies needs is to be compared with a senseless murderer of millions.

"I don't know" was all I said. Lame.

She turned to go to her class, but then she turned back around to face me. "Your mother is so desperate, she hides butter to put on her toast."

"Well, your mother is so skinny, she uses a Cheerio for a hula hoop!"

"What are you talking about?"

"I have no idea! What are *you* talking about?" I shouted into the now empty hallway.

"I'm talking about how your mother eats her toast at the sink, so you won't know she's putting butter on it—real butter, from the milk of live cows. She keeps it hidden in your fridge, in an empty Arm & Hammer Baking Soda box."

"You're making that up!"

"And one time she came into the restaurant, and my mom said your mom ordered a club sandwich. A real one," she said.

The bell rang, but Mary and I were stuck in a stare down—like we used to do when we were in second grade.

"You look away first," I said.

"No way," she said. "I always win at staring contests. You know I'll stand here all day if I have to."

"You're going to miss class. Don't you have some big new words to learn? Some more As to make?" Dang, those were supposed to be insults, but they sure weren't sounding like them. I had a lot to learn in the whole game of fighting.

"Okay, on the count of three, we'll both look away. Agreed?" she asked.

"Agreed," I said. And, without losing eye contact, I walked just close enough to her so we could shake on it.

"Okay, get ready," she said. "One. Two. Thr—"
She stopped. "Ha! I won! You looked away. I won!"

"You cheated," I exclaimed, refusing to look at her again and risk starting the whole thing over.

"That's not cheating. I deceived you. There's nothing wrong with deception, Ferrell Savage."

Just then two guys I barely knew came down the hall. "Hey, you're the Golden Hill survivor dude," one of them said.

"Cool shoes," the other one said.

I thanked them and then looked at Mary, to show her that some people recognized cool when they saw it, but she was already halfway down the hall and walking through her classroom doorway.

I *click-clacked* to my own classroom, half-completed homework in hand, mumbling to myself about Mary, kites, lightning, tornadoes, cramps, and pirate- and shark-infested oceans.

Chapter Fifteen

Race is on

I WAS LATE TO SCIENCE CLASS AND STILL ONLY
had half my homework. I quickly prepared to tell
Mrs. Beaker I couldn't find it. Which wouldn't really
be a lie, after all, because when you forget to finish
your homework, it is hard to find. But before I had
a chance to explain, she smiled and winked at me.
"You're fine, Ferrell," she whispered, and indicated a
seat toward the back.

There were some parts to this whole hero business I was going to miss.

Then, when I *click-clacked* to my seat, Jack
Coolahan stood up, so he could see my feet better.

"Hey! Are those Big Bertha Spikes?" he asked. The whole class tilted in their seats to get a better look.

"Yeah," I said.

"I didn't realize you were a golfer as well as a sled racer," Mrs. Beaker said.

"I'm not either one, actually," I answered.

Several kids nodded their approval of my shoes. I even heard Jack saying he was going to wear his golf shoes the next day.

I took the empty seat across from Littledood. "Hey," I whispered when I sat down.

He kept his gaze straight ahead, as if he hadn't heard me, so I tapped my foot toward him. I dropped my pencil in the aisle. I even went, "Psst, Littledood." Nothing. So I tore off a tiny piece of paper, wrote "Race is on" on it, and tossed it toward him. The little ball of paper hit him in the hand and bounced smack-dab in the middle of his desk. But he didn't budge.

As I watched, his eyes turned slowly down toward the top of his desk. He carefully opened the paper wad with the same hand that had been hit. Barely moving at all, he flattened the paper with two fingers, appeared to read it, and in one quick swoop, he tossed the paper into his mouth and proceeded to chew it up and swallow it.

He sure was dedicated to drama and secrecy.

After class, when everyone was shuffling around and getting their assignments together, I said to Littledood, "Hey, what did you do all that for?"

"I'm afraid I don't know what you're talking about," he said. And then he pulled me by my sleeve to a quiet spot and whispered, "It is in your and Mary's best interests not to tell anyone of our arrangement."

"Leave Mary out of this," I said. "You can't prove she's related to Bell."

"Oh, indeed I can. Marital documents and birth announcements are easily available at the courthouse. I can produce all kinds of proof on who Mary is." Littledood sneered. "Now, listen, I have agreed to honor your and Mary's secrets; I expect you to honor mine and not tell anyone I've given you an ultimatum. My win will be more magnificent to the crowd if they believe you feel the pain of your defeat."

"What if I win? You'll tell everyone?"

He laughed. "You won't win. But, to answer your question, no, I wouldn't tell."

"Let me make sure I have this clear: If I lose, the secret is safe, and if I win, the secret is safe," I said.

"Simple as that. All you have to do is come down from the top of the mountain with your Pollypry and show everyone you've made a gallant effort. I will then bask in the glory of my win. I couldn't have offered you a better deal. Well, a better deal as far as blackmail goes." He chuckled.

"Who's going to be there to see us come down?"

"Every kid in town will be there. Don't you worry. Just leave that up to me."

"But Specter Slope isn't even a sledding hill. Why can't we race down Lakeside Ski Hill? It's right next to Specter and just as long. Plus, they have special days just for sledders, no skiers."

"That's too easy," Littledood said.

"I don't understand. You won the trophy. The trophy! What else is there?" I asked.

"I'm braver than you, I'm smarter than you, and I built a better sled. I want all of Golden Hill to recognize me for the awesome that I am—so, we've got to do this big."

I opened my mouth to tell him that glory and recognition are overrated. But before I could get the words out, he said, "You will meet me at Specter Slope on Saturday at ten o'clock, or I tell everyone that your great-great-great-uncle ate Mary's—"

"Okay." There was no talking him down. "I'll be there."

Chapter Sixteen

WHEN I GOT HOME FROM SCHOOL, THE POLLYPRY was leaning against the wall in the mudroom at the back door.

"I found it on the front porch," Mom said. She sat at the kitchen table writing up a grocery list. "There was a note that said 'Good luck,' and then in small letters at the bottom it said 'Eat this note after you read it.' Well, I didn't eat the note, but if you'd like to, it's on the counter." Then she smiled at me and said, "You're up to something, aren't you?"

"Yes," I said. It was nice having a mom who

didn't pry into my business. Being honest with her came much easier that way.

"Do you want to talk about it?" she asked.

"I can't," I said.

She nodded. "Okay," she said, and went back to her list.

I went into the mudroom and examined the lounge-sled. It looked pretty good, actually. The aluminum frame had a dent in it, but that wouldn't interfere with my comfort or with its speed down the slope. One ski had come loose and needed to be reattached, and the webbing in the entire middle was frayed and torn up. It would have to be replaced with something . . . but what?

"Can I get you anything from the grocery?" Mom called out from the kitchen.

Duct tape! That would fix it! I could reweave the middle of the frame with duct tape, doubled up on both sides so I wouldn't get stuck to it.

"I'll need lots and lots of duct tape. And super-glue, too," I said.

"What about Mary? Do you think she needs any-thing?"

I could tell Mom was suspicious. This was as close as she would come to getting into my business.

I hid my emotions behind a face as blank as I could muster up, and with as smooth a voice as I could force, I said, "Mary's not coming."

"Oh," she said. She came to the mudroom door and waited a second for me to explain. But when I didn't, she said, "I guess she went home after school?"

"How am I supposed to know? I'm not in the business of taking care of her. That's your job." I tried not to sound irritated.

"Well, actually, last year Ms. Vittles, Mary, and I had a discussion about that. We all agreed Mary is responsible and reliable enough to stay home alone."

"Then why does—or did—Mary come over every day?" I asked.

Mom shrugged. "Because she wants to, I guess. She's very fond of you."

Ha. She's fond of torturing me, that's all. Good riddance.

On Saturday morning I told Mom I was going to hang out with the guys and maybe do some sledding. I grabbed four fruit pies and a family-size bag of Skittles and put them in a plastic bag for a snack on the hill. The way I figured it, I would catch the nine thirty ski bus to the top of Lakeside Ski Hill; that would take about twenty minutes. Then it would take another ten minutes to hike across the ridge to Specter Slope. I'd meet Littledood, and then we'd head down, have his little hoopla celebration, and I could be home in time for lunch. Deep-fried potato skins smothered in veggie chili and soy cheese, with a strawberry-banana-cashew smoothie loaded with a few extra spoonfuls of brown sugar. I already couldn't wait to get home.

When I reached the bus stop, the bus was already there. The door was open, and I looked up at the driver, who sat in his seat, chugging a big can of Energeeze Me drink. He burped and then smiled down at me. "Well, come on," he said. He didn't look old enough to drive.

I squeezed past the door and up the steps with my sled and tripped over a snowboard that lay on the floor next to the driver.

"Can't you find a better place for that?" I asked.

"Yeah, I know of a better place. But do you know how hard it is to drive with your feet on a snowboard?" He laughed hysterically and held out his hand for my money. I gave it to him, and he checked out the Pollypry. "Haw, dude," he said. "I know who you are now." He bowed his head toward me and said, "It's an honor to give you a lift, Survivor Boy." And he laughed hysterically again. No more *Energeeze Me* for this guy, please.

"Why is the bus so empty?" Maybe I was the last one in town to learn that getting on a bus with a driver juiced up on sports drinks was taking a bigger health risk than any I'd yet taken in my young life.

"I reckon folks aren't hard-core adventurers like you and me. They get scared when they hear any mention of a little snow coming over the mountains."

"A little snow?"

"You know how it goes. They say the mountains are going to get dumped on, and then the snow peters out right when the clouds get to Lakeside." He sighed and added, "We never get the good blizzards."

Now, there're two words you don't usually hear together: "good" and "blizzard."

I took a seat toward the back, thinking it would decrease my chances of being hurled through the windshield. I leaned the Pollypry sideways in the aisle. The bus started, the driver shut the door, and then he suddenly opened it again. Mary leaped up the steps, breathless. She handed Mr. Energy her money, then, seeing me in the back, she took a seat in the front.

"What is *she* doing here?" I mumbled out loud to myself. But I knew what she was up to. She didn't think I could handle it. She was scared I was going to somehow blow it and her secret—and mine too, let's not forget!—was going to be spilled all over town.

The bus rolled forward. It crawled out of the parking lot and began to trudge up the hill. "Woo-hoo!" the driver shouted. "We're on our way now!"

At this pace it would be noon before we got there, but you know what? I could not have cared less.

Just looking at the back of Mary's head, I felt a surge from years' worth of aggravating situations. Like the way she never gives me the answers to our homework assignments because she tells me I need to understand it for myself. I understand everything; it just takes me too long to do it. And when we go to the SuperTarget with Mom, Mary pulls on my shirt-sleeve when I start to wander down the wrong aisle. Maybe I want to look at something. Besides, isn't getting lost the whole reason for cell phones?

Oh, and here's the big one. When we're sitting on our beanbag chairs in front of the TV, she always turns to look at me during the funny parts. I used to think it was because she wanted to make sure I was having a good time. But now I get why she does it.

"Hey, Mary!" I yelled from the backseat. "I know

why you look at me during the funny scenes on TV."
She turned around. Her face was small and pinched
up underneath her teal-blue hat. "It's because you
want to make sure I'm not too stupid to get the jokes."

"If you get SpongeBob's jokes, then why do I
always have to explain them?" she yelled back.

Low blow.

"Boys and girls," the driver said. He shook his
head and wagged his finger over his shoulder at us.
"This is a happy bus."

"I'm not talking to you!" Mary shouted at me,
and jerked herself around so fast, the bobble on her
hat got twisted up.

"Me neither!" I shouted back, which didn't really
make sense.

Oh, who cares? The bus chug-chugged on, and
we rode in silence. I leaned my head against the window and felt the vibrations rattling my brain. And
then I tried to remember why I was doing all this to
begin with.

Oh yeah, because of redemption.

Redemption is for suckers.

Chapter Seventeen

WHEN THE BUS STOPPED AT THE TOP OF THE mountain, I heard Mary ask the driver, "Which way is Specter Slope?"

He pointed. "Just follow that ridge. But whatcha going to Specter Slope for? Nobody skis or sleds there. Even young adventurers like Survivor Boy back there know better than to go to Specter Slope."

"Why? Avalanches?" Mary asked.

"No, man. Worse than avalanches. Trees."

Well, then, I had all the information I needed now to go back home and enjoy a Saturday of cartoons. But just then Mary looked at me and said, "You can cope with a few trees."

"Arghh," I said to myself. I grabbed my sled and dragged it up the bus's aisle, bumping it against all the seats as I passed.

When Mary and I finally reached the top of Specter Slope, Bruce was reading a book.

"Sorry we're late," I mumbled.

"An hour and a half late," Littledood said. He closed his book, *Much Ado About Nothing* by William Shakespeare. "I wasn't worried. I know you both have a lot riding on that sled, no pun intended." Then he chuckled. "Okay, the pun was totally intended."

I looked down the steep slope and heard Mary's snarly voice in my head saying, *You can cope with a few trees*. The mountain was so dense with pines that there wasn't even a trail to follow!

"How are we supposed to get around the eight hundred trees between here and the bottom?" I asked.

"Well, I don't know how *you're* going to get around them, but I'm going to steer my way. Like this." And he showed Mary and me how the steering bar on the front of his sled moved with barely any effort from his feet.

Show-off.

"Surely you didn't forget to build a steering device into your sled," Littledood said.

I didn't answer. I set the Pollypry next to the Titanium Blade Runner and comforted myself with the thought that this would all be over soon. I played with the duct tape repair job to show Mary I knew what I was doing this time. Strong and solid. Phew. I sat down, adjusted my legs, and prepared to push off.

"Are you ready?" Littledood asked.

"Yep," I said.

"On your marks," he began, "get set—"

"Hey! Ferrell, you are not ready!" Mary screamed from behind us.

"GO!" Littledood shouted. But neither of us moved. Littledood looked at me, and Mary ran to my side.

"You can't stop me now!" I protested.

"What are you thinking?" she shouted into my face. "Am I just going to walk down the slope?"

"I don't know! I guess I figured you would take the bus back. You're responsible for your own self, Miss I'm-So-Independent-I-Don't-Need-to-Go-to-Your-House-Anymore."

"No! I'm going down the slope with you, on the Pollypry."

Littledood stood up from his sled. Mary and I stopped fighting.

"You're quitting? We can go home now?" I asked.

"No. Carry on with your bickering. I seem to have dropped my bottle of oil for the steering bar. You go whenever you're ready."

"You mean I can begin without you?" I asked.

"He did already say 'go,'" Mary pointed out. But she stood in front of me and put her foot on the Pollypry to keep me from sliding.

"Yes, that's right. I said 'go.' Consider the head start a little gift from me to you." Littledood smirked.

"I don't need your little gift," I fumed. But Littledood ignored me and walked along the path back toward the road.

"Take it, Ferrell. We need all the help we can get." She took her foot off the sled and stood to the side.

"What's this 'we'? You're not coming," I insisted.

"Yes, I am. I have to. Who else is going to make sure you don't kill yourself like you almost did last time?"

"But you're the one who's making me do this in

the first place," I said. No, wait, I was doing this to redeem myself.

"I already thought you were dead once. We all did. How much can we continue to rely on miracles?" She slid onto the back of the Pollypry and continued to talk. "Thank you for doing this race in order to preserve my integrity and to maintain my reputation as an intelligent human being. It really is the least you can do, given that it was your great-great-great-uncle who ate my great-great-grandfather. Now, as my own act of goodwill in support of this situation, I will not let you die." She looked behind us toward the path along the ridge. "Oh, and one more thing." She pulled the real Polly Pry's quill feather out of a side pocket in her ski pants and stuck it in a grommet behind her at the back of the sled. "I stopped by your house this morning."

"What for?" I asked.

"I guess I must have known you'd forget *something*. Now let's go before Littledood gets back." Then she wrapped her arms around me. "This is not a hug, by the way," she said.

Maybe not, but I still felt my insides kerplam into a gazillion shards of giggling kissy-faced yellow marble pieces.

I pushed off down the hill, and away we went, gliding across the snow, the wind in our faces, our scarves blowing behind us, and the world belonging to Mary and me. I could hear *The Ride of the Valkyries* in my head as we sailed along.

Then *slam!* We jolted to a stop.

"One tree down, seven hundred and ninety-nine to go," I said. I didn't even try to hide the big, goofy grin on my face.

Chapter Eighteen

ONE HUNDRED AND FIFTY TREE SLAMS LATER,
Mary and I started to get the hang of turning.

She called out instructions from behind. "You lean
hard to the left, and I'll go only lightly to the left. Now
lean forward! Lean forward! Farther!" I felt her lean
way back. *Crrunch*. Instead of hitting the tree head-on,
we skimmed the side of it, hard enough to spin us
around and come to a stop. Near success!

"Yahoo!" we both shouted.

"We need more weight in the back," Mary ordered.
"Let's switch places."

As we stood up and brushed snow off ourselves,

I looked up the hill. No sign of Littledood. Without thinking, I reached into my pocket, searching for a sugar-glazed fruit pie.

"Hurry. Get back on," Mary commanded.

"Do you think he could have passed us somehow?" I asked.

"Maybe he got lost," Mary said. "Come on! We could have a real shot at winning this thing if you'd just hurry it up!"

"But I'm hungry and . . . Oh no . . . Aw, crud! When you stopped by my house this morning, you didn't happen to grab my bag of fruit pies and Skittles, did you? I must've left it on the kitchen counter."

"No, I didn't. You're better off not consuming anything than putting that junk into your body. Eat some snow and let's go!" Mary said.

I grabbed a handful of smooth, stomped-on snow and bit into it. After a few mouthfuls, my tongue went numb and my teeth hurt. But at least it helped me forget the emptiness of my stomach. I sat down behind Mary and wrapped my arms around her. Something small and happy inside me said, "Woo-hoo, you're hugging Mary," but something bigger and monstery said, "It could be hours before you get something to eat."

After about an hour had passed, and somewhere between thirty and thirty thousand more trees had been bonked, I was done. I was sick of eating snow, sick of cold toes, and sick of sledding. Now it was beginning to snow. We had reached a level place on the hill and had to walk the Pollypry. I tied my scarf around one end and pulled the sled behind me. We were getting close to the bottom, I knew, because I could see the Specter Slope skating pond off to our right. A few summers ago I had hiked up the slope with my dad and we'd fished at the pond. We had eaten macaroni salad and corn chips with spicy bean dip. Now a strong wind was picking up, and flakes were falling, but I hardly noticed. Mary and I walked without talking, and I kept my focus on putting one foot in front of the other.

"Do I hear your cell phone ringing?" Mary asked.

"No. It's my stomach. It's growling."

"That's crazy loud!"

"Now you see why I have to eat every two hours." I caught a faint whiff of smoke, and through the snow, which was falling harder now, I could barely make out a small shack.

"That must be the shelter for the skating pond," I said. I could imagine a family inside, taking a break from skating, drinking hot cider and eating toasted marshmallows. "Maybe we could head over there and rest for just a minute?"

"No. It would take us four or five minutes just to get there. We can't spare the time," Mary said. She trudged on. "We're close to the bottom."

"If we're so close, then why should we hurry? Don't you think the little dude's just tapping his fingers waiting for us?"

"Look, if we have to be losers, let's at least make it as close as we can," Mary said.

I stopped walking, and the scarf slipped from my hand and fell to the ground. My body didn't care about making Mary mad.

"Oh, for Pete's sake. Rest. Just for a minute, though, and right here," Mary said. "We're not hiking all the way to the shelter." I sat down on the Pollypry. Was Mary glaring at me or squinting into the falling snow? I was too tired to guess. "You know, people can go days without eating," she said.

And with that, she pulled out a chunk of beef jerky and chomped down on it. My mouth watered, and I felt slightly dizzy. I wanted to push her face-first into the snow. Hunger will do that to a guy. I lay down on the sled, closing my eyes and trying to find a picture in my head that didn't have food in it.

That's when the flakes really started to fall. Hard. I sat up, but I couldn't even see the skating shelter anymore.

"Hey, the Weather Channel said it was going to be clear all day," Mary said.

"They were wrong," I grumbled into the wind. I wasn't sure if Mary could even hear me, so I said more loudly, almost yelling at her, "Since when does anyone put that much faith in the Colorado weather report?" The wind whipped around us, and snow was coming down harder with each word I spoke. I stood up, and Mary moved closer to me, as if there were something I could do to stop the snow.

"Ferrell! I can't see in front of us . . . or behind us!"

It was as if someone had dropped white buckets over our heads. I grabbed the Pollypry off the ground and shouted to Mary, "Hold on to my jacket! We can't just stand here. We've got to keep heading toward the bottom of the slope."

"But how do you know we're going the right way?" Mary asked.

"I don't!"

She hung on to the back of my jacket, and I took a few steps forward and hit a tree. We could get really lost if we kept walking, so I came up with an idea that could at least help Mary.

"Face the tree and crouch down," I told her. I felt her let go of my jacket. "Are you as close to the tree as you can get?"

"Yes!"

I turned the Pollypry lengthwise. The black of Mary's jacket and her teal-blue hat were just visible, and I could tell she was pressed up tight against the tree. I shoved one end of the lounge securely into the snow and pushed the other end against the tree and over her head. I took off my coat to fill in the gaps in the webbing. It wouldn't keep her snow free, but it would help.

I curled up low, facing the tree, and pressed as close to it as I could get. As long as I kept contact with Mary, I knew I wouldn't lose her. One step away, and I might never see her again.

"Ferrell! Where are you?" Mary's voice was frantic.

"I'm right here!" I shouted. I tried to reach for her, so she could feel how close I was, but I decided to keep my face covered with my arms instead.

"We're going to die, Ferrell!"

"No, we're not. We're just going to be scared for a while, but we won't die."

"How can you know that?" she screamed at me.

"Because I'm the Survivor Boy, remember? And you're with me," I said.

Chapter Nineteen

THE NEXT THING I KNEW MARY WAS HITTING ME.
Smacking me all over.

My head was tucked tightly under my arms, so
at least she wouldn't be able to give me a concussion.
I tried to uncurl my body from under the tree, but I
couldn't move. I was barely able to lift my head to see
that the snow and wind had died down. I could see
a little farther ahead of us than before. Mary hadn't
been hitting me. She was knocking the snowballs off
my hat, my shoulders, and my arms.

"You look like the Abominable Snowman. And
your lips are purple." Mary wasn't making fun; she

sounded scared. "Where's your jacket?"

I looked up and pointed with my ice-coated eyeballs to the top of the Pollypry. Mary turned and grabbed my jacket from its makeshift roof position and shook off the snow with all her might. The feather, still stuck in the grommet, was bent in half and frayed, like it belonged to a swan that had been half eaten by an alligator.

"Look what you've done to yourself! Are you crazy? I would have been fine." She continued brushing the snow off me, brushing and smacking a little harder than she needed to.

She pulled me slowly to my feet and forced my stiff arms into my jacket sleeves. "Are you all right?" she asked.

I wanted to say, *I'm fine, so fine that I can't even feel anything at all, which is kind of cool, but it makes it hard to move,* but I didn't quite have the lip action to get out those words. Then when I tried to nod, I realized my neck and shoulders were shaking too hard. So from the only warm and properly functioning spot in my whole body, probably near that spot where the marble was lodged, I managed to muster up enough strength to say, "Uh-huh." I hoped it was loud enough to be heard.

"You've got to move around, Ferrell. It's the best thing for you. Get your blood going. Come on, let's start walking."

My arms had now wrapped themselves tightly around me, and all I wanted to do was curl up into a ball.

"Come on! Pump those arms." She grabbed my left arm and lifted it up and down, up and down. She was going to break me!

"Now walk. Let's go." She pulled the Pollypry a few steps ahead of me, but I couldn't get my legs to work.

As soon as she noticed I wasn't following, she stumbled back to me. She slid the sled up behind me. "Lie down," she ordered. "I'll pull you to the shelter. We'll get there faster."

My brain argued and said I didn't need to lie down, but the rest of me didn't agree. Mary put her arms around me and sort of tipped me over onto the sled. I closed my eyes and lay there, feeling myself being pulled.

I heard a door unlatch and felt the skis scrape across something rough and hard: the concrete floor. The shelter. We had made it. The air was warm, and as soon as the door clanked shut, all I could hear was

Mary's breathing. I opened my eyes, and her worried face hovered over mine. I tried to smile to show I was okay.

"I'll help you up," she said. "The hearth is still warm from a fire here earlier."

She put her arms around me, pulled me to my feet, and half carried me to the fireplace. I wanted to make a joke and say, *Is this a hug or are we dancing?* But I still couldn't get the words out. Before she lay me down on the hearth, she took my jacket off me, then put it over me as a blanket. She rolled up her own jacket for me to use as a pillow. The coals, which were barely smoldering, had a sleepy campfire smell, and the warm bricks heated my back the way a hot concrete pool deck bakes you after you've jumped out of a freezing swimming pool. I finally stopped shaking so hard, and my world felt a little less like an earthquake.

The shelter was made of logs and was about the size of a one-car garage. Some light came in through two windows. Mary pulled a wooden bench up next to me and sat down.

"I almost killed you. You almost died—again!— because of me," she whispered.

But after my first so-called near-death accident,

a lot of people told me about what happens when you come to the edge of death. And, once again, none of those things had happened. I hadn't seen a white light, my dead relatives hadn't called out to me, the hands of Elvis hadn't reached for me. I didn't have the energy to say all that, though, so I went with "Nuh-uh."

"Are you comfortable?" she asked, tucking my jacket underneath me, like a blanket around a mattress. "There must be more I can do for you. Oh! I know! Water! You must need water. I saw a bucket outside. I'll fill it with snow, and you'll have water to drink in no time." She bolted out the door, leaving a cold flurry of air behind her, and quickly returned with what looked like an oversized white snow cone.

"Do you want me to feed you some now?" she asked.

"I'm good," I said.

"Oh, Ferrell, I'm so sorry. I shouldn't have put you in this position. Everything I do turns into a failure!"

"Science fair," I argued.

"Ughh, don't remind me. Second place! How shameful!"

"Council vice president," I whispered. Why couldn't Mary see how amazing she was?

"Exactly!" She stood up and stomped around the room. "When I didn't win the presidency, that's when I suspected I was on the same losing streak as my relatives. The plug popping out of my sink made it official. I should have known coming with you today would only lead to a catastrophe. You must hate me for being so awful!"

"I don't," I said.

"Well, thanks a lot! That just makes me feel worse!" she yelled, and plopped herself back down on the bench next to me and stared at the floor. "I do these awful things to you, and you just go on liking me! At some point, it just feels rude."

I was flabbergasted. I wanted to say that out loud, so Mary could hear me use the word, but my poor brain was so twisted up that I started to laugh instead. It came out as a long wheeze, which startled Mary at first, but when she realized I was in hysterics, she folded her arms and scowled at me. Then, finally, she laughed too. Soon she was laughing so hard that her nose squeaked, and tears streamed down her face.

At last we caught our breath. She said, "You always have fun, don't you? I mean, here you are, half dead, frostbitten, and starving, and you're laughing your head off. You didn't even want to be here, or do the race at all, but you did it for me, to protect my secret, and you show no resentment toward me."

She stopped talking and waited for me to respond, but I didn't know what to say. My brain was thawed now, thanks to the hearty laugh, but I was at a loss for words.

She leaned over me and spoke softly. "Are you tired? Do you wish I'd shut up? I promise I won't be mad if you say yes."

"Keep talking," I answered.

"I know this is going to sound dumb, but you know what I was thinking about when we were huddled around the tree during that whiteout? I was remembering how in first grade, Miss Cowl would pass out juice boxes at snacktime. She always had orange or grape or lemonade, and when kids fussed about the flavor, she'd say, 'You get what you get and don't throw a fit.' Man, that lady got on my nerves! But the thing is, no matter what flavor you got, you'd pick it up, slurp it down, and say, 'This one is my favorite.' I had thought it was just a food thing for you, but you're like that about everything. You just roll along, not worrying about winning or making good grades or being the best."

She paused, and I wondered if she was going to start yelling at me for being lazy again. But she didn't. Instead she said, "I wish I could be more like that."

My face burned, but I managed to say, "Thanks."

"You know," she went on, "maybe if I could be more like you, I wouldn't be such a loser. Maybe I don't have to hate my dad for being stupid and leaving us. I mean, Mom and I are doing okay, right? Maybe the way things turned out is my favorite way, because, well, any other way and I might not have gotten to spend so much time with . . . I don't know . . . you."

I was tingling from head to toe, and I wasn't sure if it was because of her words or because my blood was coming unfrozen. I blinked and kept listening.

"There's something I've been wanting to tell you. I think you're—"

Brr zzz brr zzz . . .

Mary jumped. "Is that your stomach again?"

"My cell phone," I said.

"You've had a cell phone all this time? Are you kidding me? I could've called for a helicopter and had you flown out. Where is it?"

I'd hoped she'd ignore it. Whoever it was, they'd call back. Besides, I'd only brought the phone in case of an emergency, and, in my opinion, being half dead, frostbitten, and starved in a shelter with Mary, who was about to confess some kind of feeling for me, which I think was probably going to be pretty awesome, was no cell phone–worthy emergency.

She reached into my coat pocket and pulled out the phone.

Throw it out the door, Mary. Just throw it!

"Hello?" she asked. She listened for a few seconds, then looked at me and said, "It's Littledood!"

"How did he get my number?" I asked.

Mary shrugged. "What?" she yelled into the phone. "You're talking too fast, slow down!" Then to me she said, "He says he's had an accident."

Chapter Twenty

"WHAT HAPPENED? OH MY GOSH . . . YOU'RE where?" Mary ran to the window and looked out. "Well, we're nowhere near there yet. We haven't even seen a skating pond," she lied. "You must have gotten way ahead of us. . . . I'll ask Ferrell what he thinks, and then we'll call you. . . . Yes, as soon as we can."

She came back to the hearth, and I struggled to sit up. Mary was smiling big.

"You're never going to believe this. Come here, let me show you something."

She stooped down, and I put my arm across her shoulders and hobbled with her to the window.

"Look way over there on the other side of the pond. See that big mound of snow near the edge? Underneath it is Littledood's Titanium Blade Runner, which apparently broke through the ice and got stuck. See that little wooden outhouse? Littledood's in there. Trapped by all the snow that fell in front of the door."

We stood at the window, my arm across Mary's shoulders, looking at that outhouse. We laughed and laughed until something occurred to me: I was ravenous. There was no way I'd be able to find the energy to walk over there and help dig out Littledood, even with Mary's shoulder to lean on.

We hobbled back to the hearth, where I sat upright.

"Are you okay?" Mary asked.

"I'm definitely warmed up and a bit looser." I rolled my shoulders and my neck. "I'm still achy but pretty much fine, except for one thing: I'm starving."

Mary brought me the bucket of melting snow, and I drank with my cupped hands. I wished we had some Kool-Aid to pour into it. Water is so boring and useless without sugar.

My phone buzzed again, and Mary looked at its face. "It's Littledood again." She handed the phone to me. "Don't answer it. He'll just keep bugging us. You should turn off your ringer."

I pressed the buttons to make the vibrating stop and stuck the cell phone back into my pocket.

"You're still pale, Ferrell. In fact, your face is gray," Mary clarified.

"I don't feel so good. But we have to help him. The sooner we get him out, the sooner we can get this whole race over with. I'm sure people are already waiting for us at the bottom of the hill."

"Well, they're going to have to be patient. We'll go when you're feeling better."

But without food I was only going to feel a lot worse.

"You know, I've been thinking," I said. "I can see how it could happen. They were lost, there was no food. They were all going to die. Alferd Packer ate everyone because he was hungry. What else could he do?"

Mary's eyes got big, and she scooted away from me.

"I'm pretty sure I'm not going to eat you, Mary."

"Pretty sure? That's the best you can do?"

"Quite sure. Almost positive," I tried to assure her. "If anything, I'd cut off my own arm and barbecue it for you."

"Wow," she said. "That is so sweet of you." She shifted closer again. "I wonder why there are so many movies about vampires and none about cannibals. They're both gross, no matter how cute the guy is who's biting you."

"True. Good point." She squeezed her thigh through her snow pants. "There's some grade-A quality meat in there."

"I've noticed that when people eat meat, they have to take small bites and chew a lot. But I bet you'd be tender. Easy to chew," I said.

"Really? You think so?"

"Oh, I do. I've purposely never considered it until now, but yes. You know how people eat fried chicken right off the bone? That's how I'd eat your leg, Mary."

"Why, thank you, Ferrell. That's the nicest thing anyone's ever said to me."

I laughed. I always had the most fun with Mary, when she wasn't getting all fancy with her words and showing off how smart she is.

She reached deep into her coat pocket and pulled out four string cheese sticks and an opened bag of beef jerky. She held them out to me. "It wouldn't be the end of the world if you ate an animal product. Just this once," she said.

I shook my head. "No. I can't. It's too risky. Especially right now, in the state of starvation I'm in."

"If you're really starving, then this is the time to break your vegan rule. What are you afraid of?" she asked.

"I've never told anyone this before," I said, "but whenever I smell a hamburger or watch my friends eat bologna in the cafeteria, my mouth starts to water in a serious way. I have to swallow a lot just to keep from drooling."

"Sounds normal, although maybe a little extreme . . ."

"It can't be normal. I'm afraid if I try even a small bite, it could stir up some crazy monster in me. Even before I knew I was related to Alferd Packer, I've imagined that if I ate a chicken or a cow or an egg, I'd turn into a werewolf, go on a rampage, and eat the entire population of Golden Hill."

"You wouldn't. Think about it: You're starving right now, and I basically just offered you my leg for a barbecue sandwich, but you didn't take it. You let yourself imagine it, but you didn't go all monster about it. You wouldn't do it, Ferrell."

I thought for a moment. I reached for a piece of string cheese, then pulled my hand away.

"Wow, this is really difficult for you," Mary said. "Okay, I have an idea." She scooted back onto the hearth and pulled up her legs and crossed them. She sat up straight and held her hands palms up, with her middle finger touching her thumb. "My mom says when I'm feeling uptight or stressed out, I should try this."

I crossed my legs, straightened my stiff back, and held my hands the way she had hers. I closed my eyes and sat there.

"Why are we doing this?" I asked.

"It will help clear your head," she whispered.

"Are we meditating?"

"Yes," she continued to whisper.

I waited.

"I don't get it." I didn't know why, but now I was whispering too. "Is something supposed to happen?"

"Breathe in. And then breathe out," she said.

"That's what I've been doing my whole life."

"Let your thoughts go. Let your mind be blank."

"Got it," I said.

"Focus on the blank space between your thoughts."

"That's easy. For me, it's harder to focus on the thoughts between the blank spaces," I said. "I guess I've been meditating all along."

I opened my eyes and reached for a string cheese stick. Mary opened her eyes too when she heard the plastic crackle as I peeled it apart. I bit into the cheese.

"Thanks for taking care of me," I said with my mouth full.

"No problem. It's a pleasure to serve you," she said.

"And I hope to have a chance to serve you, Mary Vittles."

Mary rolled her eyes. "Serving Merry Vittles. It sounds like a cookbook."

Chapter Twenty-One

"SO, WHAT DID YOU THINK OF THE CHEESE?" Mary asked.

"Chewy. Salty. Pretty good stuff." I patted my stomach. "I feel kind of full. But you know what would really taste good right now? A bag of Skittles."

"You eat too much junk food, that's your problem. You're in a constant state of a sugar crash."

I stood up and stretched my arms and legs. "I'm actually feeling really good now. Maybe we should get a move on."

We stepped outside with the Pollypry. Mary

bent over and gently tidied up the frayed feather pieces, trying to get it to stand up straight.

"The rachis is broken," she said sadly.

"The what's broken?" I asked.

"It's the shaft in the middle of the feather. This is a flight feather, probably from a swan," she added.

Wow, Mary Vittles might just be the smartest girl in the world. I was proud to be stuck in the snow with her.

She tried one more time to straighten the feather, but it bent back down. "Oh, well. I think we should leave it attached to the Pollypry, anyway."

The clouds were splitting up, and patches of blue were showing. It was like a whole different day from when I'd been dragged on the sled, lying flat on my back. Now I wanted to beat on my chest and yell like Tarzan. Instead, I simply breathed in the fresh air.

The skating pond was wide, but from where we stood, we could see that the mound of snow covering the Titanium Blade Runner was still there. And the door to the outhouse was still shut. As we made our way through the deep snow around the pond, my mind began to wander.

"Speaking of outhouses . . . ," I said.

"Who was speaking of them?" Mary asked.

"Well, we're walking to one, so that's kind of the same as speaking of it, don't you think?"

"No. But go ahead. What about them?"

"Well, I was just wondering. Back in the olden days, what would people say if a kid went to the bathroom in his pants? Would they say, 'Hey, that kid just went to the outhouse in his pants'?"

"That's disgusting," Mary said.

"It's kind of a weird thing to say, anyway," I continued. "I mean, if a kid poops in his pants, he obviously didn't ever go into a bathroom at all. Right?"

"I guess that's true," Mary admitted. "People should be more accurate in what they're trying to say."

"You're here! Finally!" A voice came from the crescent moon window in the outhouse door. "Did you all stop at Disneyland on the way down or what?"

"Poor Littledood. Aren't you having fun in there?" I asked.

"Start digging. Get this door open! I'm about to pass out from the smell in here!" he yelled.

"How ungracious. We're here to help you. You could at least say 'please,'" Mary said.

A big brown eye appeared in the middle of the moon window. "I've been in here since the beginning of that squall. That was two and a half hours ago! I'm not saying 'please.'" Littledood banged on the door. "Just open it!"

Beyond the trees, past the outhouse, I could see a clearing all the way from the top of the mountain. "Hey! There's a perfect sled run right there!"

The eye in the moon disappeared, and it was suddenly very still and quiet in the outhouse. And then it dawned on me. We'd been duped by the little dude!

"Hey, you lied to us. You led us down the wrong hill. You didn't go back to look for a bottle of oil you'd dropped. You waited for us to go first, so you could go down the real hill! You cheated!" I shouted.

Silence for a few seconds and then finally Littledood said, "Okay. Yes. I cheated."

I picked up a snowball and threw it against the outhouse door. "Can you believe this guy?" I asked Mary. "We hit all those trees for nothing. We could have been finished with this whole crazy race hours ago."

I scooped up another snowball, and just before I threw it, Mary put her hand on my arm and squeezed my jacket through her mitten. "Ferrell?" Her face was serious. "It wasn't all that bad, was it?"

My hand opened up and let the snowball fall

back to the ground. I knew exactly what she meant. "I guess it wasn't my worst day ever," I said.

I turned back to the outhouse door. "So, Littledood," I said more calmly this time. "Tell me, if we let you out, what would happen next?"

"We'll call off the whole thing. I'll never tell your secret. Please! Just get this door open!"

"What do you think, Mary? Should we call it off and just go home?"

"I don't know. We've come this far," she said.

"True," I said. "And, well, who knows? We could still win. Weirder things have happened."

"Let's finish it," Mary said.

"Are you sure?"

"Absolutely!"

"All righty." To Littledood I yelled, "Looks like we're going to finish the race. But all of us on the real hill this time, starting from here. No cheating, Littledood. Agreed?"

"Agreed!"

Mary was never one to give up on anything. And as much as I couldn't wait to get home and have a root-beer-and-frozen-coconut-milk float, I did not want to be a quitter either.

We dug and dug the snow away from in front of

the outhouse until we worked up enough heat that we had to unzip our jackets and take off our hats. When we finally cleared the last bit, the door burst open, and Littledood fell to the ground at our feet.

I looked down at his face. It was a little green. I guess that's what happens when you spend so many hours closed up in an outhouse.

"Mary and I will go find a starting spot. You dig out your sled."

Mary and I walked out toward the slope—the *real* slope meant for sledding and skiing, that is. Mary stopped suddenly and looked down.

"Whoa, it's steep here," she said.

"Naw, it just looks steep because there aren't any trees," I said. But the truth was, it did look like quite a drop; not quite like the Tower of Doom ride at Elitch Gardens, but almost. Luckily, at the bottom, just before coming to a road, the slope leveled out. I was pretty sure it was all safe. Or at least safe enough . . . pretty much. Okay, I was a little nervous.

A snowplow had already come by and cleared the way for cars after the squall.

"Yeah," Mary said doubtfully. "It just looks steep without trees."

We stood there in the quiet of the newly fallen

snow, looking down. I wasn't breathing, and I couldn't tell if Mary was or not. The silence was interrupted by the muffled sound of music down below. As the music grew louder, we heard laughing and screaming. A double-decker multicolored psychedelic bus rolled up the mountain and stopped right at the bottom of the slope.

"It's the Lakeside party bus," Mary said.

"And they're more than an hour late," Littledood growled as he came up from behind us. "I'll have to ask for a partial refund for that."

"You're kidding! You paid for a party bus?" I asked.

"I told you we'd have an audience, didn't I? Inside that bus are one hundred and twenty of our school-mates. Let's hope they all brought their cameras, so they can share the experience with those who didn't sign up in time."

The doors to the bus opened, and out spilled tons of kids carrying balloons and making noises that sounded like they were blowing party horns. I swear I could smell cupcakes, even though I was about the equivalent of four blocks away.

"Man," I said, "I hope someone thinks to save me a Coke."

As Mary watched, her eyebrows scrunched together. "We're about to make fools of ourselves in front of the whole school," she said.

"They're just a bunch of kids." Right after I said that, the Channel 7 news van pulled up with a camera crew. "Okay, a bunch of kids and everyone else in Colorado. But that's all."

Mary took a deep breath and held her chin up. "It'll be fun, right?" she asked me. But her question had the same doubtful tone as when she'd ask me, "Did you do your math homework?"

"It's going to be a blast, Mary," I assured her. "What's the worst that could happen?"

She didn't have a chance to answer. Littledood slid his Titanium Blade Runner up next to the Pollypry. "Looks like a good enough starting spot to me," he said, and sat down on his sled.

Slowly Mary situated herself at the front of the Pollypry, and I plopped down behind her.

"You all go whenever you're ready, and I'll start afterward," Littledood said. He took off his glove and examined his fingernails. "It doesn't matter to me. I know I'll still have to wait for you at the bottom."

Mary's back went stiff with anger. "Oh yeah? That's what you think, you arrogant, conceited, egotistical—" And before she could get out her next insult, Littledood tossed his glove aside and pushed off. With a swift *sha-wiiiing*, he was on his way.

"Hey!" I yelled. "You said—"

I didn't even have my arms around Mary when she leaned down and pushed off with all her might, thrusting herself and the Pollypry forward while throwing me backward and into the snow.

I sat up just in time to see the terror on her face as she looked back and screamed, "Ferrell! Help me!"

Chapter Twenty-Two

I SCRAMBLED TO MY FEET AND BOLTED DOWN the hill, but Mary and the Pollypry were flying ahead. She pulled her legs from their sitting position to a lying position, flattening herself facedown on the lounge.

It was an awesome maneuver! She held herself flat, and the Pollypry looked sleeker than ever, the broken feather flapping in the wind behind her. Littledood was in the lead, but not for long.

Mary gained on him!

Mary was ahead!

Mary was going to win!

"Ma-ry! Ma-ry! Ma-ry!" the crowd screamed for her.

"Go, Mary!" I yelled. I couldn't wait to see her face at the end. She's no loser, that's for sure. For once *I* was going to say to her, "I told you so." Golden Hill would talk about it forever. Vittles versus Littledood—the classic tortoise and hare story.

Until . . . just past halfway down, Mary and the Pollypry were suddenly airborne. To this day, no one knows how it happened. Did she hit a mound of snow? Was it an ice patch? A sudden strong wind? When she landed, she was still hanging on, but the head of the Pollypry hit the ground first, and then the back flipped up, causing her to do a full-on cart-wheel, sled and all!

I ran faster down the hill.

Mary rolled and spun, and at times I couldn't even tell which was her and which was the Pollypry. They were a blur of color—teal-blue hat and silver duct tape. At last they tumbled to a stop. Mary lay flat on her back in the snow, with the Pollypry on top of her and the bottoms of the skis pointing upward, like the legs of a dead dog on its back.

The cocky little dude won. He swerved to a stop and, still sitting on his sled, raised his hands over his head. But when no one ran to greet him, he jumped up, waved his arms around, and shouted, "I won! I won!"

But the swarm of kids ran past him and up the hill to Mary.

I got there first and was scared to touch her or to say anything. Her hands still gripped the sides of the lounge frame, and her feet were locked up tight on the end. Her face was smushed into the webbing, and her eyes were closed. I was sure she was dead.

"Oh, Mary, what have I done to you?" I asked. I knelt down next her.

She opened one eye and looked at me. I leaned over the sled, so my face was close to hers.

"Were they making fun of me?" she asked.

"No. They were cheering for you."

Her other eye opened.

"She's alive!" Jerry Dunderhead shouted, and the crowd cheered. "It's a miracle!"

I slid the Pollypry from Mary's determined grasp. She had a checkerboard imprint on her cheek when she peeled her face from the webbing. She sat up, and the crowd went wild. They hooted and hollered, and when I helped her to her feet, they chanted again, "Ma-ry! Ma-ry! Ma-ry!"

"We were sure you were a goner," I said.

Mary turned to me. "Oh my gosh! Ferrell! I'm invincible!"

"Well, no, you're not. We can all see you. But you're pretty amazing to have survived that roll down the hill! You're a true survivor, Mary!" She wasn't exactly a winner, but I was able to say, "You're not a loser. I told you so."

Mary smiled at me. Then she turned to her fans and raised her hands over her head in victory.

Chapter Twenty-Three

MARY AND HER MOM JOINED US FOR DINNER, and Mary and I told them almost everything that had happened that day, sparing them some of the scary details. When they went home, it was late. I sat on the couch, dozing between Mom and Dad. As my eyes closed and my head fell over onto my mom's shoulder, I rehashed the events of the day: I had almost frozen and starved to death; I'd eaten cheese without turning into a monster; Mary had said, "My downhill debacle was exhilarating!"; Littledood had had his moment of glory; our secret was safe and soon to be forgotten. It had been the best day ever.

Now my belly was full after a great dinner. I was wishing I had the energy to go to the kitchen and refill another plate with leftover Save-the-Cluck egg-less quiche, topped with Spare-the-Oink fake ham, along with baked sweet potatoes smothered in Soy You Think It's Butter, when Mom leaned toward the TV, taking her shoulder with her and leaving my head to fall behind her onto the seat of the couch.

"Look, there she is!" Mom cried out.

Dad pulled me up by my sleeve. "Wake up, Ferrell. Mary's on TV."

I sat up and rubbed my eyes, just in time to see the teal-blue-and-silver cartwheel spin down against a white backdrop on the TV screen. Knowing she was alive and safe in her home made that spill down the mountainside a beautiful sight. Amazing.

"Wow! Such a thrill to watch! Folks, that was Mary Vittles, a brave little soul from Garfield Middle School." The camera switched to the Channel 7 newscaster, the eternally tan Steven Stowick. Mary and I sometimes stayed up to watch the news, just so we could try to catch Steven Stowick's eyebrows move. They say he hasn't moved anything on his face, except his lips and eyeballs, since 1998.

"Unfortunately," Steven Stowick continued, "we

weren't able to get past the crowd to Mary Vittles for a comment. But look who insisted on joining us tonight: her competitor, Bruce Littledood."

The camera panned out, and there, sitting next to Steven Stowick at the news desk, was the little dude.

"Oh, bless that boy's heart. He sure wanted to be on TV, didn't he?" Mom asked.

Littledood smiled big with his red chapped lips. He wore a bow tie and his hair was slicked back smooth.

Steven Stowick looked into the camera and said, "What do you say we watch that footage again in slo-mo. Roll it, Sam." Television viewers all over Colorado watched Mary slowly twirl like a lounge-sled ballerina while we heard Steven Stowick say, "So, tell me, Bruce, what did you think when you saw your opponent"—he let out a single-syllable chuckle—"quite literally flipping out?"

"Clearly, it takes a genius to build a sled like my Titanium Blade Runner, plus a great deal of time and effort." Littledood's words came out stiff and sounded rehearsed. No doubt he'd been practicing this spiel for weeks. "But the construction of such a vehicle is only half the battle. To be able to maneuver and control such a sled, you—"

"Watch this! There she goes, landing on her back, with her beach chair on top of her. Oof! And she's not even hurt! Brava!" Steven Stowick clapped his hands when the clip ended. "Brava!" he said again as the camera brought us viewers back into the studio with him and Littledood.

"Now, tell us the truth, Bruce, were you terrified for Mary's well-being?" Steven Stowick asked.

Littledood straightened his tie and stared into the camera. "The key to my win again today was to stay focused on the task at hand. And I'm sure you noticed I said that I won *again*, because, of course, it was with my Titanium Blade Runner, which I built with my own two hands, that I won"—Littledood paused for a moment—"the Big Sled Race on Golden Hill."

Finally, Steven Stowick got Littledood's point. "Well, I'll be darned. I didn't realize you'd won on Golden Hill. I'd love to talk to you more about that, but we're just about out of time. How about if we watch the footage of Mary Vittles one more time, and you can tell us what it feels like to compete against such a resilient, brave young heroine. Sam, are you ready to roll that clip again?"

My dad slid to the edge of the couch. "Yeah, I want to see it again," he said.

But Littledood stood up and slammed his trophy onto the desk. Steven Stowick, who was really only capable of three subtle expressions—kind of happy, slightly sad, and almost concerned—now looked up at Littledood with his eyes popping in confusion.

"Don't show the clip," Littledood demanded. "I won the race. I am the winner!" He walked around the desk, stood in front of the camera, sneered, and said, "Ferrell Savage and Mary Vittles, congratulations. You've managed to do it again." His face was so close, I could see the hairs in his nostrils. My mother gasped and threw out her arm to protect me, like she does when she's driving and comes to a sudden stop.

"Well, this time you two are not going to get away with it," he said, snarling. He stepped back, and I hoped he was finished, but he wasn't. "I have something to tell the world about Savage and Vittles."

"Cut to a commercial!" I yelled at the TV.

"Savage confessed that he turns into a werewolf and that he may go on a rampage and eat the entire population of Golden Hill."

"Hey! How'd he know that?" I shouted.

Mom pulled her arm away from me and put her hand to her mouth.

"Whoa, that's not good," Dad mumbled.

"And that's not all . . . ," Littledood continued.

"Enough! Get him off the screen!" I yelled. "Someone please shut him up before he says anything about Mary!"

"Oh, dear, we are out of time—" Steven Stowick interrupted.

But Littledood kept going. "Ferrell Savage came this close to cannibalizing Mary Vittles today."

I jumped off the couch and grabbed the sides of the television. "Nooo! That's a lie!" I exclaimed. "How does he know that?"

And as if he'd heard me, Littledood held up his cell phone. "I have it recorded right here, and I can play back their whole conversation."

Littledood was pulled away from the camera while Steven Stowick tried to regain control of his newscast.

"And now let's switch to our segment on how to get brighter, more vivid colors for your Easter egg dyeing. . . ."

Littledood disappeared. Maybe Security carried him away or maybe it was one of the cameramen. Either way, it was too late. The damage was done.

Chapter Twenty-Four

I LAY IN BED, STARING AT THE CEILING, WAITING for the sun to come up. What's an acceptable hour to go to the home of the girl you love and whose life you've just ruined? I wanted to beg her forgiveness, but it was a stupid idea at any hour. I rolled over onto my stomach and buried my head under my pillow. She'd never forgive me. I should just move away. No, I couldn't abandon her. I needed to help her get through this. She hated me and would probably never speak to me again, but still, I had to convince her she wasn't a loser.

"Because she's not!" I yelled into my mattress.

I replayed the conversation Mary and I had had

in the skating pond's shelter; I tried to recall when I might have bumped my phone, causing it to call Littledood. If only I could remember exactly how it had happened, I could go back in time and undo it.

I pulled my pillow off my head and looked at the clock. Six o'clock. I reasoned with myself. How about I wait two hours and then go knock on Mary's door? Eight o'clock for Mary on a Sunday morning was reasonable. Besides, if she'd seen the news last night, she probably wasn't sleeping either. If she hadn't seen it, then I'd have to be the one to tell her.

I rolled out of bed, went to the bathroom, got a glass of water, listened to some music, drank the water, closed my eyes for a while, went to the bathroom again. . . . Finally. It was eight o'clock. I stood up, but my feet wouldn't move toward the door. I fell backward onto my bed.

I couldn't do it.

But I had to.

I took a deep breath and tried again. I jumped out of bed, slipped my bare feet into my Converse, and grabbed my jacket. Just as I was about to head out the door, I realized Mary was likely to become upset and start using big words. So I grabbed my pocket dictionary off the living room shelf.

I rang Mary's bell, and she answered almost immediately. She was dressed in a soft, blue sweater and unfaded jeans; and her hair was slightly damp from showering. She looked at me and smiled. Ugh, she must not have seen the news.

"You have penguins on your pajamas!" she said. She burst out laughing.

I looked down at my flannel legs and smacked myself on the forehead. Oh, well. It was too late to save my own face. At least she got a good laugh to start the rest of her downhill day.

"Are you sleepwalking, Ferrell? You look like a zombie." Mary was still laughing when she closed the door behind me. I stood in the middle of her small living room and tried to think of how I was going to tell her. Littledood's mapped-out speeches were actually a pretty smart idea. I sat down on the love seat.

"Seriously, are you okay?" she asked. She sat down next to me.

"I am. Yes. But I'm afraid you're going to be really mad at me, and I'm willing to sacrifice the life of my cell phone if you want to smash it and bury it deep underground . . . and me along with it."

"It's okay, Ferrell. I know what this is about. I saw the news."

"Littledood? You heard what he said?"

"He's a twerp, but you gotta give him some credit. He didn't exactly go back on his deal and tell our secret. He didn't mention Alferd Packer or Shannon Bell."

"No, I guess he didn't," I said. I hadn't thought of that. "But he told them our conversation about how I was afraid I'd turn into a werewolf, and he made it sound like you were almost my first victim."

"He kind of twisted our words," she said. Then she shrugged. "It's not as big a deal to me as I thought it would be. But what about you? Are you embarrassed he told the world your biggest fear?"

"Huh. I never thought of it as something I didn't want people to know. And especially now that I'm pretty sure—almost certain—I'm not part monster, I feel okay about it."

"Right. See? That's what I've been thinking about a lot lately."

"That I'm not a monster?"

"Well, no, not that exactly." She slid back into the couch and curled her bare feet up under her. "I was thinking about how you deal with circumstances. And how you don't let other people's judgments affect you. Like your big survivor moment on Golden

Hill and how you became the local modern-day living legend."

"Uh-huh," I said, not sure where this was going.

"And everywhere you went, everyone practically bowed down to you, kissing your toes, acting like you were a king or something."

"No one ever kissed my toes," I corrected her.

"And in all of that, you never got bigheaded. You never acted like you expected to be treated differently and you never got conceited and all show-offy about it."

"But what does that have to do with Littledood being on TV and nearly exposing your family of losers? Uh, and remember, 'losers' is your word, not mine."

"Because . . ." She thought for a minute. "Remember that day I first told you about my ancestors?"

She was referring to the day of the hug that wasn't a hug, but I still think it was.

"Kind of." I tried to sound cool.

"Well, you said my dad was stupid because he left us. And you know what? You're right. That is what makes him a loser. My dad's family made stupid decisions. And now I've finally figured out why: They thought with their brains, not their hearts."

I nodded. I kind of got what she was saying. "Your great-great-grandfather thought with his brain until my great-great-great-uncle ate it."

"Your way of thinking is better, at least most of the time. And as long as I have you around, I'll remember not to be ruled by my brain. You're a role model, Ferrell."

My stomach growled loudly. "Sorry. It was the word 'role.' It makes me think of a roll with . . . mmm . . . with cinnamon and a sugary glaze. I haven't eaten breakfast yet."

Mary jumped up and grabbed her shoes and socks by the front door. "Go home and eat breakfast, then meet me at Spinelli's. We're scheduled for an exclusive interview with the *Golden Hill Times*. I'm going to tell them about our family history. Yours and mine, if that's okay with you."

"You mean everything?"

"Everything," she said. "I think it's cool our families have made it into history books. It makes an interesting story, don't you think?"

I had an idea, but Mary was going to hate it. I stood up and walked slowly to the door, wondering if I should even suggest it. "Hey, Mary, what if we ask Bruce Littledood to do the interview with us? He knows the history even better than we do, and, well, because of us, he has kind of been cheated of his fame."

Mary's shoulders dropped, and then she was quiet for a few seconds. "Okay," she finally said. "He's obnoxious and insufferable, but you're right."

"I'll call him. Then we'll meet at Spinelli's in half an hour," I said.

"Oh, and Ferrell?"

"Yeah?"

"Don't forget to put on clothes, okay?"

I looked down at my flannel jammies. "You got something against penguins?" I asked. I pushed my toes out, flattened my arms to my sides, and waddled out the door.

I loved the sound of Mary's laugh.

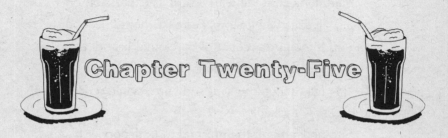

Chapter Twenty-Five

I WAS THE LAST ONE TO GET TO SPINELLI'S.
Ronny Meddle from the *Golden Hill Times* sat at the
counter with a cup of coffee. He fiddled with his beard
while reading from a piece of paper, and Littledood
stood in front of him, bouncing on his tiptoes, getting
ready to explode like a soda that's been shaken in its
bottle. Mary read over Mr. Meddle's shoulder.

"What's going on?" I asked.

Littledood pushed back his shoulders. "It's a
report I wrote after my dad and I did the research on
Alferd Packer."

"It's good," Mr. Meddle said. "With just a few minor

changes, I'll be able to print it. It will be a nice historical piece to go along with the sled race article. How would you like to have your own byline in the newspaper?"

"Awesome!" Littledood practically squealed.

Mary looked at me with a serious expression on her face. "It's our whole story, Ferrell. Bruce Littledood wrote up the entire account of our sordid history and ends it with a commentary about you and me."

"He tells about how you and I are related to Bell and Packer?" I asked.

She nodded and then turned to Littledood. "It's a well-written article, Bruce. You did a good job."

"I know. I'm pretty much an expert on—" Littledood stopped himself. "I mean, thank you." And then to me he said, "Thanks to you, too, Ferrell, for giving me this chance. I'm really sorry for telling the whole world about how you're afraid you'll eat everyone in Golden Hill. But I explain in the article, right here"—he pointed to the typed pages—"that while Alferd Packer did suffer from terrible indigestion for the rest of his life, cannibalism has no effect on the health or sanity of future relatives."

"Cool!" I said. I was already starting to feel less monstery. "But what about clearing Mary's reputation? Is there any way you can tell our history without making

her family look like a bunch of losers? Maybe work it
into the article that even really intelligent people sometimes get eaten and that it's not a sign of stupidity?"

"He does better than that," Mary said. She picked
the typed article up off the counter. "Listen to what he
says:

> "'Let the record show that yesterday,
> Bruce Littledood defeated Ferrell Savage
> and Mary Vittles once again in a great
> downhill race, because clearly he built a
> stronger, sleeker, and higher-performing
> sled. But here's something that won't
> show on the records. Ferrell and Mary
> each wiped out on the Pollypry in dramatic
> fashion. Splattered on the hillside, they
> should have been embarrassed, humiliated,
> and broken in spirit. But instead they
> defined their games. Like real heroes, they
> played by their own rules. If we learn one
> thing by studying history, it's that heroes
> like Ferrell and Mary define themselves.'"

"Wow," I said. "So you think we're heroes?"
"That's what I said," Littledood answered. "But,

remember, my name will still be on the trophy."

"As it should be. You won fair and square," I said.

"No hard feelings, then?" He looked first at me, then at Mary.

"It's all good," Mary said.

Mr. Meddle had some questions for Mary about yesterday's race and her near-death experience. Afterward, the photographer took a photo of Mary and me with the Pollypry, and one of Littledood with his trophy.

As they said their good-byes and thanks, Littledood followed the newspaper men out the door, saying, "If you want to take more pictures, I can show you the way to the site of the Packer massacre. In fact, I know where all the historical sites in Colorado are."

"Well, now, I could sure use a guy like you on my paper staff," Mr. Meddle answered.

When they were gone, Mr. Spinelli announced to his customers, "The *Golden Hill Times* special edition will be on sale next to the cash register by four o'clock this afternoon."

And to Mary and me he said, "How about a couple of free root beers for my favorite indestructible patrons?"

"Yeah! Free root beers!" I shouted.

At last, Mary and I were alone at the counter, sitting on our stools, drinking our root beers.

"Are you having fun being the Golden Hill Survivor Girl?" I asked.

She smiled. "I'm amused."

Outside Spinelli's, I could see a few people stopping to admire the Pollypry leaning against the front window.

"And to think, none of this would have happened if it weren't for Polly Pry's quill pen," I said. "You know, she didn't even actually use a quill pen to write her stories."

"How do you know?" Mary had a doubtful look in her eye.

"I read it on the Internet. She only used it occasionally, for dramatic effect."

Mary laughed. "I learn something new from you every day."

That's when I reached over and put my hand on top of Mary's. She didn't yell at me, she didn't fling me away, and she didn't call me a name. She didn't even seem surprised.

"Do you still have the yellow marble I gave you?" she asked.

I put my free hand on that spot just below my heart and above my stomach. "Yep. I keep it in a safe place."

Author's Note

Alfred Packer, also known as Alferd Packer, and Polly Pry are true, historical figures. I recently had the pleasure of visiting Lake City, a lovely town nestled in the San Juan Mountains in Colorado. The people who live there are warm and friendly and they enjoy sharing what they know about the history of Alferd Packer. Most of the information I used in this story came from the Hinsdale County Museum.

If you'd like to learn more about Alferd Packer and the events took place in 1874 on that winter day near the wild-west town of Lake City, you can find books and articles about them at your local library as well as hundreds of websites on the internet. If you decide to do the research, you may discover that there are contradicting theories about the details of what happened. Some stories will say that Packer murdered his five traveling companions before he ate them, and other stories will have you believe that he was in fact not their murderer.

At any rate, it goes without question that Packer did indeed consume the flesh of the men, which enabled him to survive the seventy-five mile hike to the Los Pinos Indian Agency.